BRING ME MY BOW

BOOKS IN THE SEQUENCE OF

SONS OF THE MORNING

VOLUME ONE

A STORM OF CHERRIES

VOLUME TWO

DANCING DAYS

VOLUME THREE

THE LAST ENCHANTMENTS

VOLUME FOUR

A TOUCH OF THE SUN

VOLUME FIVE

BRING ME MY BOW

BRING ME MY BOW

SIMON WATSON

WORDWISE
PULBOROUGH • WEST SUSSEX

BRING ME MY BOW

• VOLUME FIVE OF •

SONS OF THE MORNING

First published in 2010 by
WORDWISE
Brambles, Batts Lane, Pulborough RH20 2ED
Tel: 01798 875413
Email: wwordwise@aol.com
www.wordwisebooks.co.uk

ISBN 978-0-9553401-4-7

Cover Design by Ian Tyrrell
Book Design and Typesetting by Michael Walsh
Typeset in Galliard and Caslon Open Face

Printed and bound in Great Britain by
ASHFORD COLOUR PRESS
Unit 600 Fareham Reach
Fareham Road
Gosport
Hants PO13 0FW

To K

CHARACTERS IN

BRING ME MY BOW

Mr Bendinck, Headmaster of Talbot College, Berks.
Johnny Clarke, protagonist (1-4)

EATON HOUSE ST BOTOLPHS

Mr Oakes, Headmaster (1)
Fay Palfreyman (Mrs), secretary
Mr Paget, master
Mr Long, master
Bett, cleaner
Mr Feast, verger of St Botolphs
Mrs Box, aggrieved passer-by

RAWLE

Lord and Lady Nidd (3)
The Hon. John (Onjon) Nidd (3)
The Hon. Fiona Nidd (3)
Cousin Rupert (3)
Mrs Brydon, cook; Frith, butler, and other staff.

OUTRAM PARK

Val Treviso, remedial teacher and Johnny's mentor
Norman Brewster, Head of English
Chalky White, teacher
Ma Boardman, Joint Head

Mr Baker (Half-Baker), Joint Head
Danny, reluctant learner
Abel, rowdy Jamaican boy
Eddy (Mr Eddington) former charismatic headmaster
Pilch, difficult boy

CLOUDS

Menzies Arkwright (MA; Minkie), 'Hed'
Stella, Tom, Sebastian, Rupert, Chris, Robbie, Anna-one, Anna-two, Lily, Freda: the members of Johnny's tutor group
Mrs Fawkus, Mops and Mrs Pinne; matron, laundrywoman and seamstress
Mr Pickles (Prickles;The Hedgehog), a senior member of staff.
Mr Murphy, deputy head

The bracketed number after a name signifies appearance in a previous volume of the *Sons of the Morning* sequence:

1	*A Storm of Cherries*	*(set in prep school c.1957)*
2	*Dancing Days*	*(set in public school c.1961)*
3	*The Last Enchantments*	*(set in Oxford 1962-3)*

CONTENTS

1

TALBOT COLLEGE 1

The curtain rises on the study of the Headmaster of Talbot College, Berkshire. The lights come up to reveal an old-fashioned conventional box set of a large room with large furniture, one corner occupied by a large desk on which are large piles of papers. They have the look of documents that ought to have been read, haven't been, but might be now that term is over.

On either side of the empty fireplace, its mantelshelf thick with trophies and cards, are two armchairs. Opposite it is a sofa. On the sofa is a black spaniel. In each chair is a man. Both wear suits. The elder of the two, evidently the headmaster, has the build of a wing three-quarter. He is almost completely bald though scarcely middle-aged and his head gleams with candour. He is at ease, almost sprawled, his right ankle resting on his left knee, exposing canary-yellow socks between brogue and Duke of York check. The younger man, his suit of clerical grey, sits upright as though on the alert if not actually on his guard. The older man is smiling as he talks; the younger is choosing his words with care. The older, toying with his pipe, is aiming at a fireside chat; the younger is determinedly being interviewed.

All about them is the soft silence of an empty school. Through the window and on the far side of the drive can be seen a solitary groundsman attending to an exhausted cricket square.

'And so how did you enjoy yourself at Oxford?' enquires the headmaster breezily; with five hundred and twenty reports now all done, he is almost light-headed with fatigue and relief.

The applicant has no blue to offer, no first, no memorable role with OUDS, no speech at the Union. In fact he had hardly played games, just done a bit on the river in the Cardinal

College boat, had scraped a second and set not a foot upon any stage. Like most undergraduates he had spent much of his time socialising with college friends, mismanaging an inadequate love life and trying not let himself down too shamefully in tutorials. Oh, and getting his fingers burnt (literally) in a Cuban Missile Crisis demonstration. None of that, he realises, will strengthen his application, an application he feels weakening at every turn. When asked to talk about his sporting interests he has, in desperation, blustered about 'outdoor pursuits', a concept that has the headmaster narrowing his eyes.

'I'm very interested in the pastoral side,' declares our candidate. 'Pastoral' is vague enough and no qualifications required there. 'So I'd like to assist in a boarding house.'

'Good,' smiles the headmaster, reaching into his jacket pocket for his tobacco pouch. 'Good.'

He's no fool this man, for all his appearance. He is evaluating this – his one and only – candidate for the post of Assistant English Master as follows: Clarke, John Clarke. A fairly presentable young man who speaks properly, has been to a decent public school, an even more decent Oxford college and has had some experience of the classroom as a volunteer teacher in India. He now has a year's experience of teaching in a variety of schools in England but he has no training. The question is, how will he fare in a double lesson with a fractious Upper Fourth at five-thirty on a dreary late-November evening? In addition, he has nothing particularly strong to offer in any field, but the headmaster realises he cannot be choosy. Is anyone better going to turn up out of the blue in mid-July to fill a post in September?

The headmaster taps the residual ashes from his pipe into the huge glass ashtray on the table between them and says nothing. Give the boy his own opening, see if he comes up with anything. In the silence both men look at the dog which raises its greying muzzle and slopes off the sofa to sit upright at its master's knee, panting lightly, as if offering its services. John Clarke – Johnny to all who know him – wishes the dog would come over to his side. Instead it looks at him with a quizzical expression.

'Of course I'd like to help out in any way,' says Johnny to the dog, 'but to be honest my real interest is education.'

It would be an exaggeration to say the headmaster looks surprised, let alone taken aback, by this assertion but there is a stilling of the fingers round the nicotine-yellow oilcloth tobacco pouch that suggests that this may be an unusual topic, one that will require a moment's reflection before proceeding.

'Education, eh?' he queries non-commitally as if Johnny had named some little known oriental form of meditation – which in these neophiliac times wouldn't be at all surprising.

Johnny also is taken aback by his own statement. Since when was I interested in education? Oh well, as the saying goes, 'How do I know what I think till I hear what I say?'

The dog and its master wait politely for a development of this spontaneous asseveration. Johnny has boldly embarked upon his tightrope and must push on.

'Of course, my subject comes first – I love English – but I think education itself is a fascinating subject too, the theory and practice of it, why we have it in the forms we do, what it's supposed to achieve. What works, what doesn't. How we can improve on it, and so on...' He pauses, trusting he has got up sufficient impetus not to teeter and plunge into the chasm, hoping the headmaster will pick up the tune and sing with him. The headmaster doesn't. 'I wonder,' Johnny therefore continues, 'what the relation is between education and society, for example, which comes first and whether society should dictate the nature of education or vice versa. In India, as I discovered, it is that way round, education is all about getting qualifications. That means passing exams. So the teacher's job is to prepare his students by giving them answers to questions he can predict to a certainty by looking at previous papers obtainable in handy booklet form in the bazaar. They learn the answers by heart – or try to.'

'And regurgitate them in the exam, no doubt – or try to,' says the headmaster.

'Exactly.'

As if in approval, the old spaniel shambles over to Johnny and lies down on his shoes, collapsing with the completeness of a marionette when its strings are slacked.

The headmaster stretches his legs now, unrolls his tobacco pouch and begins to finger the contents reflectively as if about to draw the winning number. 'So there you have an educational system at odds with true education,' he says. 'Of course, it's something we have to guard against in our own system – teaching for exams – though I have to remind myself of the iffy.'

'The…?'

'Ah! an acronym of mine. The IFI, the Implicit Fees Imperative.' He smiles. 'What this means is that parents are paying and whatever else they may be looking for like leadership opportunities and the like they will want results, in the form of exam passes, that is.'

'Yes, I suppose so.'

'Mustn't forget the iffy,' repeats the headmaster complacently, tamping errant shreds of shag into his briar. 'Just as a politician forgets at his peril who voted him in so the headmaster forgets at his peril who pays for his tobacco' – he flourishes the pipe and, smiling, fumbles in the other jacket pocket for the answering rattle of matches. 'There are, in other words, certain realities' – here he extracts a Swan Vestas and prepares to strike – 'certain realities underlying the ideals to which we aspire.' He thrusts his pipe into his mouth by way of peroration.

'The question is then,' Johnny says, 'can there be reconciliation?'

'Well, do *you* think there can?' queries the headmaster through clenched teeth.

'Yes, I do actually.'

'Then how is that to be done – in your opinion? How do we inspire them with the true love of learning and make sure they pass their A Levels at the same time?'

With a sudden little rasp the match is struck and applied to the polished bowl. The flame is sucked down and flares up, sucked down and… The headmaster sits back, momentarily almost invisible behind a cloud of smoke that drifts comfortably upwards. 'Tell me how.'

The dog begins to snore.

2

EATON HOUSE ST BOTOLPHS

School is Dead (Book title) (Everett Reimer)

Finding St Botolphs was easy enough. There it was, plumb on the corner of Haverstock Hill and Eaton Drive, an ugly thing in liver-coloured brick. But where was the Eaton House bit? The board in front of the church gave details of times of services and the name of the vicar. No mention of Eaton House. Johnny glanced down at the paper in his hand, the school's prospectus, one side of cyclostyled foolscap. There were no directions.

It was then that he became aware of being keenly watched. Two small black eyes in a small white face were observing him through the September-dull leafage of a privet hedge that separated church premises from Eaton Drive.

'Er, excuse me,' Johnny called, 'I wonder if you could tell me where –' but the little man had slipped away, though not before Johnny could see that he was wearing a cassock. Could he be the vicar? Surely not. As the son of one himself Johnny knew that lurking behind hedges and peering suspiciously at innocent passers-by was no part of the priestly calling. Anyway, ugly man, ugly building. 'Eaton House' surely promised better, a spacious stuccoed villa at least.

But no. Following the building round the corner, Johnny saw the sign – Eaton House Tutorial Academy – high up, just above a flight of stone steps leading to an uninviting gothic wooden door set in a wall of the same dull red brick as the church of which it seemed to be the rear part.

Johnny checked his watch. Fine. One o'clock. Seemed an odd time for an appointment but that's what the letter said. He was just about to raise the knocker when the door opened and several boys streamed past him, not rudely but not inviting him in either. Johnny entered. Inside and immediately opposite was a stable door, its open top half giving on to what was clearly the school office. A woman wearing a green eyeshade sat at a desk typing slowly.

'Hello, I'm Mr Clarke, come for an interview.'

The woman typed on as if she hadn't heard him.

'Er, hello.'

The woman looked up, not directly at him, though, but somewhere over his left shoulder. She seemed to have an eye problem.

'I didn't hear the bell,' she said.

'I didn't see one,' Johnny replied.

'It's just by your hand.'

Johnny looked down. Running along the top of the bottom half of the stable door was a shelf on which was fitted a plastic electric bell.

'That's how people let me know they're there. I don't see very well.'

Your hearing's not so good either, Johnny was tempted to say.

'I'm Mr Clarke, come for interview,' he repeated.

'Yes, the headmaster's expecting you. He'll be with you in a minute,' and she peered round the door into the dim corridor that seemed to be the hallway to the rest of the premises. 'Ah, here he is. Headmaster, this is Mr Clarke.'

'I know who he is, Mrs Palfreyman. Good afternoon, Clarke, we'll go to my classroom.'

And Johnny knew who *he* was. He could scarcely keep the exclamation to himself : 'Major Oakes!'

'You remember Major Oakes at The Dell,' Johnny wrote in his weekly letter to his parents, 'Major Oakes, MC? After the dear old place packed up soon after I left he went, I remember Mr Victor telling me, to a crammer in London, living with his ageing mother (though he said widowed sister, as I recall) in Highgate, and here he is. He's now dropped the "Major" by the way. I couldn't believe my eyes when I met him. I almost said, "Good heavens, are you still alive!" Of course I realise that when you're young any adult is old but I suppose he was no more than in his thirties in the 1950's when I was at The Dell, and now he's only in his forties. It seems incredible to be a colleague of his rather than a pupil. He still calls me "Clarke" but then he calls the other two members of the staff by their surnames as well, as if they were boys. (The school secretary, Mrs Palfreyman, is the only person to get any sort of title.) "Ring the bell please, Paget," he'll say. "New boy coming in today, Long." I call him "Headmaster" as everyone does. Apart from his title he hasn't changed much but he doesn't swear any more as he used to at the Dell (I expect that's news to you) but he is still rather Eeyore-ish and non-commital and I don't know how well I'm going to get on with him. It's rather important that I do as there are only four of us, including him, on the staff altogether.'

Johnny wasn't sure how much, if anything, he should tell his parents about Eaton House which was a poor little place. In truth he was a bit ashamed of the job which he'd taken mainly for the money: twenty-five quid a week – not bad! Johnny's father had asked him what he would do 'now that you've got your degree, now that you've had your year abroad.'

'I might become a teacher,' Johnny had replied, trying out the idea aloud. He didn't sound very convincing to himself.

'Will you need to train for that?'

'Probably. Get a postgraduate degree, sort of thing.' Further studying didn't appeal to the twenty-two-year-old.

'Would you qualify for a grant?'

'Don't know.' But he'd better find out. Apart from the previous year with Overseas Volunteers in India Johnny had been a cost to his father from the age of seven – prep school, public school, Oxford. Yes, he was an only child and yes, there had been some avuncular legacy (that ought, however, to have gone towards the purchase of a house for retirement) but a vicar's stipend was not great and though as such it attracted bursaries things at home were tight. Even now with the promotion.

'A bishop – gosh!' Johnny's father had always been a man in black: now he was going to be a man in purple. 'Bishop of where?'

'Retford.'

'Retford!'

'It's a suffragan bishopric.'

Bang went Durham. Bang went Salisbury. And where the hell was Retford?

'There'll be a lot of expenses with the move,' his mother said, not pointedly but Johnny took the point all the same: it was time he thought of providing for himself instead of being provided for. Fair enough.

'What I'll do is get some more experience,' he declared. That would get him off his father's books anyway.

So he looked in the teaching job adverts in the *Times Educational Supplement.* Now, state or private? Private was all he knew so he'd stick with that, to begin with anyway – plenty of time to adventure later. Senior or junior? Didn't seem to be much choice, certainly not in the London area where he decided he wanted to be since that was where all his friends had gone. He'd lost the only home he'd known, in Surrey, and was certainly not going up to Retford.

'But where will you live?' his mother had asked anxiously. She was suspicious of London. India was one thing – she herself had been born there – but London quite another.

'In a flat like everyone else, I expect,' he replied, but before he got around to making any such arrangement she had fixed him up with a widow friend of Aunt Grace's who lived in a little house in a little street behind Camden Square where Johnny had a little room in the back of the basement for six quid a week including breakfast (cereals and toast only). Well, it would do for the time being while he looked around.

Johnny's interview with Mr Oakes was a perfunctory matter. 'Latin, English, History and Divinity all right then?'

'I haven't actually taught up to Common Entrance but I dare say I can give it a –'

'Of course you can. Greek?'

'A bit.'

'That'll do. Not much call for it, of course. Boys aren't very bright. That's why they're here. But a smattering of it impresses the public schools. This is your room.'

Hardly bigger than a schoolboy's study. In four rows of two there were eight desks, the old-fashioned sort with sloping lids and a hole for the ceramic inkwell, long since lost, only the old stains of faded blue-black testifying to its original function.

'No biros allowed, of course.'

The master's desk was bang up against the front row and there was just room for a chair between it and the wall. The blackboard, there being no room for the customary easel, was attached to the side wall so that the boys had to turn through ninety degrees to see it.

'Chalk's in the desk but keep it locked up. They love chalk. I think they must eat it.'

There was no decoration of any kind and only one window high up on the wall facing the blackboard. This window, gothic in design and with dusty iron glazing bars, was fitted with opaque greenish glass as if it were a temporary installation pending replacement by stained glass of a religious character. A length of frayed picture cord, threaded through a metallic eye in a quarter-light at the top, was the means of opening it.

The other three rooms – 'Mine, Paget's, Long's' – were identical, other than having no windows at all, and in a row, like lavatory cubicles. In all of them sat boys eating their lunches from plastic containers, or playing with cars. They took little notice of their headmaster and his guest other than to go quiet in his presence and he took little notice of them. Johnny smiled a bit and would have liked to talk but refrained.

These four classrooms gave on to the 'hall', a somewhat bigger space with a large window taking up most of one wall, a green-cushioned window seat running the length of its embrasure. Beneath it were storage lockers containing chess and draughts sets and the boys' personal belongings, such as they were. The room was mostly taken up with a ping-pong table, or rather half a ping-pong table, there being insufficient space for a full-size one. This made for a challenging game to which the boys had adapted well. The net (always a vulnerable piece of equipment) was actually a length of wood glued across the middle of the table and reduced in height from the norm for the sake of proportion. 'Round the table' was in progress, fifteen or so boys shuffling clockwise, picking up the bat, returning the ball, dropping the bat with a clatter for the next man and moving on round. There was little conversation among the players, concentrating grimly on the game.

'And that's the lat.' Mr Oakes pointed out the establishment's one other amenity. 'Lat' for lavatory apparently. They proceeded to the staff room, so marked clearly on the door with the addition of 'No Entry to Boys'. This was a space the size of a train compartment in which Johnny was introduced to the other two members of staff. Mr Paget, who was eating a sandwich and mending a desk pencil-sharpener, smiled and nodded; Mr Long, who was daintily eating something out of a jar, put down his fork to shake hands. Mr Oakes introduced Johnny as 'our new colleague' even though he had not been offered, let alone accepted, the post. No mention was made of their previous acquaintance.

And that was that. After attempting to teach fifty uncomprehending young Indian men and women in smelly and sweltering conditions, to sit down in a small cool room with half a dozen English boys was heaven. Thick they were indeed, but not unwilling or ill-natured; not much fun to teach but no trouble. And so Johnny settled to it.

The establishment ran on narrow and unvarying lines. Each day was the same: nine to 3.30 with a one-hour lunch break though no food was provided beyond the narrow range of confectionery retailed at cost price by Mrs Palfreyman. There were no games, no activities or clubs; for these the parents were expected to make their own arrangements. Friday was 'paper day', that is there was no teaching and all the boys sat trial Common Entrance papers. Staff were expected to mark these over the weekend but then, in recompense, only one, by strict rotation, was required for invigilation, The master sat at the ping-pong table, the boys in the classrooms with the doors open where they could all be heard if not seen, the less behaviourally reliable characters doing their papers on the ping-pong table under the invigilator's eye.

Thus Monday was 'give back day,' the week starting with an anxious gathering of boys round the noticeboard on which Mr Oakes had pinned the results. This was not just a matter of a mark and a position but a mark in brackets alongside signifying the result achieved the previous week, a figure in brackets as on a balance sheet. 'Gosh, Roszak's gone up six in Maths.' 'Two more in Latin, Young, and you'll be OK for Harrow.' 'Anyone know what you have to get for UCS?' This weekly trial and its result constituted the school's single variation on the relentless routine of going over old papers, of making that umpteenth attempt to learn what came between *ne* and *pas*, to understand why x squared plus y equalled whatever it was, to remember which king followed James I, to be able to distinguish a gerund from a gerundive – generally, in fact, to be able to jump through the hoops set up by the examiners.

'We're circus trainers really,' as Mr Long remarked. 'Dangle a herring in front of the sea lion and it'll soon learn that if it agrees to balance a multicoloured ball on its nose for a minute it gets the fish. Not that we go in for rewards, of course.' (Johnny wondered why not: wasn't he, Mr Long, rewarded for his work?) Cracking the whip was one of Mr Oakes' favourite metaphors in his grammar of educational motivation. 'Carrot be damned,' he would say, 'it's the stick they understand.' Mr Long agreed: ' Human nature is much more responsive to fear than desire.' So a battery of punitive measures was in place.

This did not include 'the stick' literally. That most time-honoured disciplinary method, beating, Mr Oakes had judiciously excluded from his arsenal of correction for the sensible reason that, Eaton House being a day school, it would be rash to send boys home weeping, for their soppy mothers to be appalled by stripes on the backsides of their tender offspring. But it was not hard to find other punishments – even prisoners enjoy minor liberties whose withdrawal can be hurtful. Thus a persistent laggard might be detained in a classroom over the lunch hour and denied the natural social pleasure of 'round the table.' He might be excluded from Mrs Palfreyman's tuck shop. He might be kept in after school; although this prolonged the working day of a member of staff it could usually be combined with some regular tutoring that was additionally remunerated. 'As if the parents weren't paying enough already,' remarked Mr Long. But then some parents had 'more money than sense', or at least more money than their children had brains.

For of course the boys at Eaton House were, by virtue of being there, as Mr Oakes had said, not bright. Many had already failed Common Entrance once or even twice to become the shame and despair of their previous establishments before moving to 'an academic environment more suited to their abilities,' as the school's prospectus had it. Several of the boys were large because over prep school age, some even past the fourteen mark and developing a growth on the upper lip that could not be ignored. Others were lethargic with an excess of academic input, bloated and liverish with force-feeding, their systems unable to absorb further knowledge or convert it to understanding. They had simply reached the limits of their capacity to learn and would be much better off doing something useful with their hands.

To cater for such unpromising academic material Mr Oakes had developed warm relations with a number of senior schools founded for the purpose. They tended to be in decently remote counties like Devon or Shropshire or Norfolk, former stately homes at the end of tree-lined avenues grand enough to mollify the father disappointed of Haileybury or Charterhouse. In such places 'the whole child' was educated, that was, with moderate emphasis on academic success (since that would certainly be little) and much on the arts (well, some of them) with perhaps the rudiments of animal husbandry at the centre of Biology or elementary bookkeeping in place of Algebra. A new subject 'Design and Technology' looked like coming to their aid. And there was always sport.

'Well, not everyone can be brainy', father might say in reconciling himself to his son's establishment that most people had never heard of. 'A practical start in life, that's what suits our Jamie.' Mr Oakes would have done some work in bringing father round to this point of view but therein lay one aspect of his business skill. Dad might have started with 'Get him into Eton, I don't mind how you do it but get him in.' Getting into Eton being clearly beyond Jamie's powers however assiduously crammed, Mr Oakes would set to work lowering the parental sights until they came to rest on a more realistic target. 'Dotheboys Hall' was his generic term for such establishments, though not of course one used in conversation with parents. He was a frequent visitor to such places, almost always in term time, and was welcomed by their principals who wished to cultivate his patronage. They were perennially in need of more boys than they had and judged it well worth wining and dining prep school heads who might give their establishments a puff with parents. Mr Oakes was far from loath to accept such hospitality, particularly should there be any halfway decent fishing in their locality as was often the case given their rural location.

Fail Mr Oakes did not, or rather his boys did not fail. Occasionally one might be withdrawn by its parents on their perceiving that he would never get in anywhere. More often a continually failing candidate would develop behavioural traits that set him at odds with the school's disciplinary ethos and then Mr Oakes would be obliged to request (if 'recommend' did not work) his removal.

The workings of Eaton House were simple. Though headmaster, Mr Oakes taught full time, leaving administration to Mrs Palfreyman who operated as bursar (both accounts and estates), school and headmaster's secretary, receptionist and telephonist, nurse, provider of educational supplies and tuck shop manageress. Crouched in her tiny windowless office, her green eyeshade protecting her defective eyesight from the glare of the single fluorescent tube affixed to the wall at barely more than head height, she was command and control.

'How can I get my window catch mended?' Johnny asked her one warm September day. 'It doesn't work.' He had taken care to ring her bell before issuing this request.

'Ask our resident handyman.'

'And who is he?'

'Why, Mr Paget, of course,' she replied with an arch twinkle.

The man's willing reaction to Johnny's polite request showed that Mr Paget much preferred such practical work to the pedagogic routine of C.E. Maths (Papers I,II and – in a few cases – III), as did of course the boys he was supposed to be teaching who would either enjoy unsupervised time in his absence (for these jobs could not all be done outside hours) or, if they were few enough, would accompany him in the operation and perhaps even participate.

Mr Oakes turned a blind eye to this loss of teaching time on two grounds, one of thrift – for if Mr Paget didn't do it he would have to pay someone else – and the other of education, for what the boys gained by this informal apprenticeship might well encourage them in the practical work for which they were much better suited than the academic. What was wrong with being a cabinet maker or a Royal Engineer? Not everyone could be barristers and accountants.

Mr Paget had fitted up his Dormobile as a travelling workshop, tools in their designated places, neatly arranged and stored on one side above where a bed might have been with beneath it a workbench complete with vice. He had adapted the kitchen side to storage with drawers of nails and screws, and he used the gas-ring as a small-scale blacksmith's furnace. It was even equipped, via the vehicle's battery, for the use of electrical tools such as a saw and a drill. This provided Mr Paget with all that was required to solve Johnny's window problem: a lightweight aluminium stepladder, replacement cord for the pull, a file to ease the rusted metal of the opening quarter-light and oil to ensure the continuing responsiveness of the hinged eye through which the cord-pull passed. He even fixed a metal bracket on the wall beneath so that the dangling cord might be secured in a figure of eight.

Mr Paget's practical skills of plumber, joiner, electrician and general handyman were in frequent demand throughout the premises but nowhere more so than in the lavatory, which was not surprising since this one facility, comprising a single sit-down WC with a wash handbasin and roller-towel, served the entire community (barring Mrs Palfreyman whose arrangements in this regard were a mystery) of some forty people. Officially visits to the 'lat' were confined to break times and lesson changeovers but this was unpractical in that it created too much pressure on the amenity and a frequency of flushing which its mechanism could not be expected to withstand. It was therefore in use more or less continuously which wasn't much better and it often broke down so that it was not uncommon for a boy to interrupt one of Mr Paget's lessons with, ' Sorry, sir, but the lat's not working.'

'What seems to be the problem this time?'

'Well, the handle's all kind of loose, sir, it just waggles up and down like a bicycle pedal when the chain's come off.'

'Um. Ballcock's probably come off its hook, that's all. Did you check?'

'Er, no, sir.'

'Well, just nip back there, Anson, lift the lid and look in.'

'Must I, sir?'

'Oh, all right. I'll come and look in a minute.'

'Well, I don't know, sir, there are two people waiting and Michaelson says he's bursting.'

'Very well, very well,' says Mr Paget, laying down algebra book and chalk with ill-simulated reluctance and leaving the room to address the problem, with 'carry on with your work, boys' thrown over his shoulder, fully aware that they will do no such thing. Mr Paget was a man of bottomless good nature of which the boys took ruthless advantage and for which they loved him.

Many a time and oft had Mr Paget lamented to Mr Oakes the inadequacy of the lavatory and the need to replace it with something more robust at least, knowing that of course 'What we need is a urinal' would be met by 'There isn't room for one of those as well', unless of course one of the classrooms were given up to that function which would mean not only the loss of customer capacity but also considerable expense with no evident benefit.

But making the best of a bad job was a challenge to which Mr Paget's generous nature rose. He had been schooled in his youth as Aircraftsman Paget stationed in deepest Lincolnshire for much of the war, his job in a freezing ill-lit hangar, to repair and refit Lancasters and Blenheims with whatever materials came to hand, with the result that he had actually come to prefer improvisation to fitting the proper item in the event that such was available. Thus many a bomber's ailerons were connected to the control in the cockpit with random bits of wire that young Paget had pliered to the purpose.

'Mr Paget can mend anything,' Mrs Palfreyman had glowed.

This soft spot she had for the man Johnny was later able to witness at a little Sunday lunch party given by Mr and Mrs Paget for himself and Fay (as both host and hostess familiarly addressed her.) While they bustled about preparing the meal – 'Church rather slows us down, I'm afraid,' apologised a cheerful Mrs Paget – Fay Palfreyman, clutching her sherry, slipped comfortably into the role of guide to the ornaments of their host's front room. This seemed to be almost a museum of wartime RAF engineering, with numerous photographs of bombers back-lit by setting East Anglian suns, groups of uniformed mechanics, arms chummily round each other's shoulders, smoking, outgrinning the death and horror underlying it all.

'Some people seem almost to have enjoyed the war,' commented Johnny.

'Oh, you mustn't think it was all fun.' Mrs Palfreyman was censorious, jealous of the image of the hero whose trophies dominated the room. 'He told me once how when the planes came back from a raid – those that did come back, that is – it wasn't always broken bits of metal you had to deal with – there were sometimes…well, you can imagine if a man is killed in the plane and…'

She left it at that, anxious both that Johnny should be aware that 'the war' was not just a *Boys' Own* jolly but also that she herself should be the sole curator of the details of the horror her dear Mr Paget had been witness to: there was a limit to how much she would share.

'Yes, he can mend anything. Such improvisation!' She was proud of the word.

Thus now there was little inside the cistern of Eaton House's old Shanks that was original, Mr Paget having either cannibalised similar fitments wherever he should have had the good fortune to come across such – he always kept a keen lookout where building works were going on: it was amazing what builders threw away – or he had made them himself. He would be ashamed to buy a cotter pin, say, and the Eaton House fitment was on to at least its third ballcock to his certain knowledge.

And it wasn't just the lavatory fitment itself that claimed Mr Paget's expertise for there was also the matter of the roller towel and the basin. One of the main issues in this whole area was cleanliness but that was not his department, that was the cleaner's, Bet's, to whom the condition of the lavatory was a constant source of anguish and complaint. As far as the basin was concerned the principal problem was soap. The first difficulty here was that the basin was so ill-designed that any bar of soap of whatever shape or size would slip off the tray part of the basin beside the tap into the bowl, sliding stealthily and inexorably into the water like a crocodile. And there – since not all basin-users could be persuaded to pull out the plug after filling the basin with water – the soap would repose, softening itself up warmly like a Turkish bather, which of course shortened its useful life considerably, especially when its plastic capabilities were explored experimentally by any boy happening upon the softened item. To combat this problem Mr Paget fitted a separate metal soap-tray just above the basin but none of the boys would use it. Consideration had been given to the installation of a liquid-soap bottle rotating on metal pins, quite a modern idea, but a vision of the gratuitous high speed whirling to which this item would undoubtedly be subjected by the boys for the pleasure of observing its blurred revolutions and in the desire to see how far its contents might be projected across the room put paid to the idea at an early stage of the project's analysis. Then there was the plug. How many times had Mr Paget been obliged to re-attach the chain to its fixing! In the end he had found a length of chain twice the normal thickness and welded it in place with his blowlamp.

That fixed it.

The roller towel problem was less easily solved. 'What do you think they do – lie down inside it?!' Mr Oakes might exclaim when summoned to witness the sight of the whole thing – towel, wooden roller, fixing plugs, screws and plaster-dust – in a dispirited heap on the damp floor. 'It's only a stud wall, that's the trouble,' Mr Paget would explain. 'I can't get a strong enough fixing into it.' He didn't mind, it was just another welcome challenge to his ingenuity. In the end he ran a huge batten the length of the wall, fixing it with bolts driven right through the uprights. On to this he attached the wooden part of the roller towel with metal brackets secured to the batten with four-inch screws. And that fixed that, though it didn't solve the problem of the uses or misuses to which the boys put the towel itself. 'Change it every day, I do,' protested Bet, 'it wants changing every *hour*!' Or even more frequently, some thought, when boys used it to get ink off their hands before trying to achieve that end with soap and water.

And then there was the graffiti problem. Generally in no hurry to apply pen and pencil to proper academic purpose, the boys were assiduous in writing anywhere else, in other people's books, for example, and on their own belongings – distinguishing your own ping-pong bat with fanciful lines, shapes and colouring had become almost an art form – and of course on the lavatory wall, staff being frequently called upon in the role of criminal investigative graphologists to identify the scribes of such effusions as 'Aubrey smells', or 'Bum, bum,bum'. Mr Oakes punished such offences, without mercy but without moralising, with a detention, a fine or a telling-off but they were to him merely part of the moral cycle of sinfulness, retribution, repentance and (it was hoped) amendment of life; they were a predictable manifestation of mankind's fallen condition, a behavioural treadmill to which the sons of Adam (particularly the younger ones) were perpetually condemned. To Johnny they seemed 'not sur-bloody-prising' as he put it to his friend Onjon one weekend. 'There's nothing else for them to do, poor blighters.'

For Johnny had soon concluded that such acts of petty

criminality were a natural response to the unremitting tedium of the academic regime at Eaton House, exacerbated by the lack of leisure facilities, ping-pong hardly constituting a rich extra-curricular diet. Another consequence of this narrow and colourless routine was the prevalence of smoking which, after ping-pong, was the establishment's principal recreational activity. In this the staff set the example, in Mr Oakes' case in style and consistency if not in quantity, as he dipped at regular but not frequent intervals into the inside pocket of his blazer for his gunmetal cigarette case which he filled each morning with ten Players, his daily ration. Mr Long smoked small cigars which the boys imitated with their chocolate cigarettes, and Bet generally had a fag hanging from the corner of her mouth. Only Mrs Palfreyman abstained.

Mr Paget, in accordance with his do-it-yourself proclivities, rolled his own, his tin of tobacco and packet of Rizla papers always to hand. The operation of making a cigarette the boys watched with eager interest, Mr Paget first extracting a single sheet of Rizla from its packet like miniature Bronco, then plucking with delicate fingertips at the moist brown shreds of tobacco in the tin – the boys were sometimes allowed to put their nostrils to its soft pungency – these shreds being carefully distributed along the length of the paper held to receive them. Next followed a fascinating stage in the manufacturing process: the inchoate item loosely constructed was entered into a Lilliputian mangle, rolled therein by Mr Paget, the revered priest of this mystery, to emerge recognisable as a cigarette, albeit a malnourished one. And that was not the end of the interest to be had, for the ignition of the finished article by one of Mr Paget's Bryant and May often started with an outright, albeit small, conflagration as the end, its delicate india-paper tube perhaps insufficiently filled with tobacco, flared briefly under the smoker's nose or a loose shred of tobacco fell out, flaming like an aeroplane shot down to harmless extinction on the floor.

The smoking habit was promoted by the unusual permission of the staff to smoke while teaching – not a common feature of a conventional school. And this perhaps explained why the boys took to it, at first unknown to the authorities, but then one day they were found out, or rather reported.

'Feast says the boys are smoking behind the board,' Mr Oakes declared in the staff room one day.

This statement conveyed nothing to Johnny. 'Feast'? What 'board'?

'Mean little man,' declared Mr Long drily, 'he's probably making it up.'

'He brought me a tin of cigarette ends,' said Mr Oakes.

'He could have picked them up anywhere.'

It turned out that the 'Feast' referred to was the verger of St Botolphs and the 'board' the wooden structure in front of it, both of which Johnny had come across on the occasion of his interview. There was no playground at Eaton House but the boys were allowed to take the dank and narrow path at the side of the building round to the front, a small open space where the St Botolph's faithful would loiter a while after a service. It being so small there was nothing the boys could do in it other than look – sometimes audaciously jump – over the low brick wall surrounding the property. Occasionally they made *sotto voce* comments at or about elderly passers-by.

So they took to smoking, tucked secure from observation inside the protective V of the church noticeboard. They were fortunate that the area was not overlooked from the Eaton House side of the building, and all that the passers-by might see would be a few pairs of legs with smoke arising from behind the board as if from a small bonfire. So the boys were safe since the master on duty wouldn't think of coming out there. 'Getting a breath of fresh air,' it was ironically called and a privilege confined to longer-serving inmates.

This intrusion into his territory was deeply resented by Feast whose bid to keep the Eaton House part of the premises quite separate from his own was renewed at every Parochial Church Council meeting and as often rejected on the health grounds that the church's youthful tenants must be accorded some outdoor amenity, however scanty. That entitlement was in the lease, declared the vicar, and there it would stay. All right for him, muttered the put-upon verger, he didn't have to paint over the rude things the boys scratched into the woodwork of the back of the board, he didn't have to put up with their sniggering insolence.

But Mr Feast was at a disadvantage in several respects. One was that, though an adult and the offenders children in an age when the latter were more in fear of the former than vice versa, he had no official power over them. Also he was small, smaller than some of those teenagers. Then, not being full-time, he was not always on hand to witness their misbehaviour or attempt any remonstration, anathematise them though he frequently did *in absentia*. The most telling disadvantage from which he suffered was his determination to have no official dealings with the ungodly establishment to which he was so unwillingly linked. But his soul churned with righteous disgust at these unredeemed imps, these mischievous heathens, whose conduct was so disgracefully at odds with the morality of the religion over whose earthly temple of St Botolphs he had the privilege and duty of guardianship. He would no longer stoop to picking up the cigarette ends of those boys who were far too young to be smoking anyway. It was a humiliation greater than he could bear.

So it was that this anguished individual was further humbled into breaking his vow of non-communication with Eaton House and remonstrating with its headmaster. His own vicar and PCC might be unsympathetic but he would bypass them and go to the man who could not in conscience condone his charges' conduct. He would surely punish them as they deserved to be punished and put this part of the premises out of bounds.

The verger of St Botolphs would not be so straightforward, however, as to call in and seek audience but instead lurked in the narrow passage connecting the educational and ecclesiastical parts of the building to pounce upon the departing Mr Oakes with his grievance.

Mr Feast had the stealthy and brittle look of a man who spends too much time alone with his fears and fancies. His smallness seemed almost a matter of choice as if it might equip him better to avoid the notice and gratuitous malice he expected of others, as well as to dart his own retaliatory sting from a place of safe obscurity. He had a small pallid face, thin black hair smarmed down, a restless and flashing eye and little white hands that itched to be fingering. The uniform of his calling was a priestly cassock, little satin buttons from top to toe. Beneath it gleamed stout black shoes with sensible rubber soles of considerable thickness; round the waist of it he wore a cracked brown leather belt with a hefty buckle.

His appearance therefore gave mixed messages to the boys. His stature and personal attributes might in themselves have invited derision and even persecution but his attire was evidently religious and supported round the middle by what one or two boys from the less humane of prep schools recognised as an instrument of castigation. They therefore held off.

To Mr Oakes, however, the man was an entirely abject specimen with whom he was happy to have no dealing; but he was obliged now to respond to Mr Feast's high-pitched salutation, to hear his grievance and to receive the fruit of several days' gleaning at the foot of the church noticeboard. The headmaster, thus confronted, did not prolong the interview by contesting Mr Feast's case or scrupulously examining the grubby and malodorous evidence supporting it. Instead he took the wind out of the righteous verger's sails by acknowledging with shame the sins of his flock, humbly relieving the religious officer of these oblated fag ends and promising penitential action on the part of the offenders.

'Just put the place out of bounds, I'd say,' was Mr Long's suggestion. Mr Long always knew what action headmasters should take but had never put this gift to the test by becoming a headmaster himself. 'That'll stop it.'

'But there's nowhere else for them to go without breaking bounds,' objected Johnny. 'It seems a pity if they can't get out at all.'

'Then what course of action do you recommend, Clarke?' asked Mr Oakes.

'Well, what about fining them? If they can afford to buy cigarettes they can afford to be fined.'

'They're not buying them, they're stealing them from their

parents,' put in Mr Long.

Mr Oakes ignored him. 'So we fine all the boys who go out for fresh air?'

'No,only the smokers.'

'And how do we know which they are?'

'Well, er...'

'Tell you what, Clarke, you identify them first and I'll decide what to do about them.'

'Me, Headmaster?'

'Well, you're Head Boy, aren't you?'

Mr Oakes almost smiled and Mr Long positively smirked into his cocoa.

As it turned out, this identification process proved quite simple, Johnny having been a school smoker himself. On their return indoors for afternoon lessons he applied the breath test to all the 'fresh air fiends' as they were known by those who didn't enjoy their privilege. Tobacco and peppermint were easily detectable and Mr Oakes soon had his suspects. These – Perlman, Spencer-Grieves, Marks and Forester – he detained after school and sat them at the ping-pong table. On a sheet of newspaper he spread the verger's testimony before them.

'Now what varieties have we got here?' he enquired blandly. 'Go on, take a look.'

The boys handled the ends gingerly as if obliged to work at a distasteful jigsaw puzzle. They put their heads together muttering glumly, and sorted the items.

'Not sure what this one is, sir,' offered Marks, holding the sample.

'Well, what does it look like?'

'Not sure, sir, Senior Service maybe.'

'Then call it that. Very well, we have Strand, Weights (workmen's cigarettes those are), Woodbines (another labourer's smoke), Piccadilly, York (never heard of them) and Players number Ten (what wretched little things) and Senior Service. Paper and pencils please, Mr Clarke.' (Always 'Mr' in front of the boys).

Johnny had become the headmaster's assistant in this operation and did as he was told.

Mr Oakes then said, 'Now write down the price of a packet of each make, divide by the number of that variety and so tell me how much each of you is to be fined.'

The boys looked blank.

'Well, who can tell me the price of ten Weights? Somebody bought them – don't tell me your parents smoke Weights.'

'One-and-eleven, I think, sir,' offered Forester cautiously, unsure whether he was thereby incriminating himself for possession of such knowledge or gaining credit for having the right answer.

'And how many Weights are there?'

'Three, sir.'

'Very well. Three into one shilling and eleven pence? You've got your pencil and paper – work it out, work it out.'

The boys put their heads together again and conferred in hushed tones. Whatever they had expected as a punishment for their offence it wasn't a gratuitous Maths lesson. Mr Oakes got up to make himself a cup of tea, leaving his assistant in reluctant charge. Johnny was uncomfortable at the boys' discomfort, unsure whether to help them or leave them to their own frowning and pencil-end sucking.

The sums were eventually completed and each boy released in turn, required to pay the duly calculated impost the following day: Forester sevenpence-halfpenny for the Weights, Spencer-Grieves ninepence for Senior Service, and so on.

'Here's the money, Clarke, kindly present it to Mr Feast with my compliments.'

'And has that cured the smoking habit?' enquired his friend Onjon.

Then Johnny related how Mr Feast, his eyes lighting up at this unexpected contribution to the St Botolphs collection plate, had discovered that he had inadvertently stumbled upon a source of revenue worth nurturing. So at the end of the following week he gathered in the harvest of cigarette ends and made a second offering to Mr Oakes, for the latter then to instruct Johnny to levy the smoking tax, this time at double the rate. After that the boys, who might have been dim but were not stupid and well able to adopt the criminal's essential tactic of sidestepping rather than challenging authority, made alternative arrangements for the disposal of the butts; Mr Feast's bitterness towards Eaton House increased and the school authorities' attention was switched to another source of concern without the smoking issue having been satisfactorily resolved.

This new concern was stealing, and the whole spectrum of larceny from outright theft to borrowing without permission. The suspects for the outright theft, which was of cash from coats, and possibly other things (boys' information was unreliable) were McKinnon, Levy, Bauknecht, Tomlinson and Aubrey.

'Rather a large field, don't you think?' said Mr Long who disdained to participate in the investigative policing that seemed to preoccupy the headmaster. In the limited sphere of his own small classroom Mr Long's control was absolute. Any merriment that might be in the hearts or on the lips of the boys as they approached his domain died as they crossed the threshold. Punctuality, tidiness, attention, presentation of homework must all be faultless. Any lapse was visited with the requirement to embark on '*j'ai, tu as, il a…*' and so on until the victim ran out of conjugations. For more serious offences out would come the dreaded phrase 'A *Frere Jacques*', which meant the culprit had to stand and '*sonnez les matines*' until allowed to stop.

'No homework, Philippe?' – instead of using surnames as customary Mr Long frenchified the Christian name, which the boys found creepy. 'Well, Philippe?'

'It was my brother's birthday, sir, we went out and I forgot.'

'Happy Birthday, brother. Now on your feet.'

Even Mr Oakes found his French master's style somewhat chilly – could a boy be made to suffer more than by singing solo in public? – but he accepted it because it got results which was, after all, 'what we're here for.'

Mr Oakes' comment now was that when it came to stealing 'it is rarely the one you think it is and usually someone you're confident it isn't.'

But in spite of setting spies things continued to disappear and no culprit was discovered. Boys were encouraged not to bring in anything of value – particularly cash – and to be sure not to leave anything overnight when early comers and late loiterers might take the opportunity to explore coat pockets unobserved.

And there was one awkward aspect of it brought to Johnny's attention by Markwell who sidled up to him privately to confess that he'd had an air pistol stolen. An air pistol! What on earth was he doing bringing an air pistol into school?

'I just wanted to show it to the other boys.' (Poor Markwell, a drab boy, anxious to impress.) He didn't know what his Dad would say when he told him he'd lost it. Johnny didn't know what Mr Oakes would say if he heard Markwell had brought an air gun to school. And of course that was why Markwell couldn't report the loss. Oh dear.

It was not just the losses but the suspicion that soured the atmosphere: when criminal acts are taking place but no criminal can be identified then everyone is a suspect.

With this atmosphere and such a regime Johnny could not be content. What could he do to improve things?

One day he volunteered to do a little painting of his room, 'brighten the place up a bit.'

'Brighten it up?' queried Mr Oakes testily as if Johnny was proposing to hang nudes. 'What on earth for?'

'Well, it'll make a cheerier environment, the boys might feel happier about working.'

'Bad idea, Clarke, bad idea.' Mr Oakes had bridled at the word 'happier'- as if happiness had anything to do with it! 'Do you know why the Victorians put the classroom windows so high up? So that the little perishers wouldn't be distracted by seeing what was going on outside, so that they would concentrate, *concentrate* on what they were supposed to be doing *inside*. No, the best thing is plainness. The odd wall chart may be all right, a map or something,' he added cautiously, reaching as far out as he was capable towards that dubious concept, the 'teaching aid' – 'maybe a map.'

Such dullness, such routine, so much brown lino, so much petty crime. How welcome half-term was, even if it was only an extra day. Off Johnny went to stay with his friend Onjon at Rawle.

Rawle: *un peu d'histoire.*

At Oxford Johnny was partnered for tutorials with a fellow student of English in his year, the Hon. John Nidd, whose family seat was not far distant. There lived his parents, Lord and Lady Nidd and their just-out-of-school-age daughter, Fiona. (Their elder daughter, Selina, had married a substantial landowner and gone to live in Dumfriesshire.) Rawle was a fine old place, the home of the family for many generations, and Lord Nidd enjoyed affecting to be embarrassed that he was a *parvenu*, having only been there since 1066 or so. There had been a crisis during Johnny and Onjon's second year at Cardinal College when it became apparent that the old estate was virtually bankrupt. The parents seemed to their children to be paralysed by this state of affairs so Onjon and Fiona moved to take matters into their own hands by declaring that there must be a revolution at Rawle if it was to remain in the family. This revolution would involve closing up or leasing some of the properties, letting the shooting and the fishing and generally converting the whole place from a family leisure amenity into a family business. He, Onjon, would leave Oxford without taking his degree and go to America to train in modern methods of estate management. Fiona, who loved animals, would abandon her dream of becoming a vet and dedicate herself to the fulfilment of this ambition. The parents were deeply shocked by this idea, Lord Nidd making sneering remarks about Woburn and the lions, and pointing to the lack of funds for such a project.

And there was a complication : the Dowager Lady Nidd, who lived on the estate in a house she had built as a bizarre replica of the big house, even down to the statues of the Nine Worthies which famously adorned its front. Being a miniature, it was known as the Dolls' House. Through her own family she had inherited considerable wealth which it was assumed she would leave to her son in the traditional way. Unfortunately she had fallen into the clutches of a quasi-religious movement called the Pilgrims to which she had not only already given considerable sums but to which she was also known to be bequeathing the remainder of her substantial assets. She was therefore *persona non grata* at the big house.

Which is where Johnny came in, for he befriended the dowager and it was through him, though with no such intention on his part, that she came to see the rapacity underlying the ideology of the Pilgrims, consequently changing her will in favour of the family, thereby on her death (which soon followed) not only saving the family seat but also providing the investment necessary for the revolutionary project proposed by the younger generation.

So work was now well in hand. The Dolls' House had been let to a city man, the hayloft in the stables had been converted to accommodation for staff, the lake in the park had been dredged, stocked and let for fishing; the shooting also was profitable. As to the house itself there was a plan for the family to withdraw from 'the new rooms' as they were called, having been added early in the eighteenth century, and confine itself to the old part, the new being set up as a sort of gallery of agricultural art and a library-cum-archive of that aspect of English life, for the place had at one time been in the forefront of agricultural innovation, one of the nineteenth century Lord Nidds being the Turnip Townshend of Oxfordshire.

The staff, who for sentimental reasons the family had been unable to part with, were put to more productive functions than simply seeing to the needs of the family. Thus, while Lady Nidd donned pink rubber gloves and did the washing up and her husband dried, Mrs Brydon concentrated on the production of her famous steak and kidney pies. These were sent in batches for sale to the butcher in Woodstock, though the plan was that the estate should set up its own stall for the sale of its own produce, vegetables and fruit from the garden, milk and eggs from the home farm, and so on. From his training in America Onjon had brought the vision of combating the soon-to-be-all-pervasive supermarket with what would be called the 'farm shop' where people could buy local produce such as eggs with the odd feather attached rather than stamped with the emblem of the Egg Marketing Board, honey from Oxfordshire bees and vegetables grown without the aid of dubious chemicals.

'We're a veritable "commune" now,' said Lord Nidd, welcoming Johnny and clearly proud of his use of the word. 'All for one and one for all,' he added, dipping into a rather different ideology. This was a far cry from his initial response to his children's proposition for the future of the family estate. 'This is not a bloody democracy!' Johnny could remember him declaring angrily.

In truth there had for years been an all-in-it-together quality at Rawle symbolised by the institution called the Moot, membership of which was automatically the right of all members of the household whatever their rank or function. It centred on the servants' hall, a spacious but almost subterranean room in the old part of the house, where staff gathered at elevenses, lunch and tea and where much of the business of Rawle and its management was conducted. There Lady Nidd, taking tea, smoking and reading *The Daily Sketch* with the others, would discuss menus with Mrs Brydon who presided over the two-handled yellow enamel teapot. There Lord Nidd knew he could catch Milton to discuss some matter relating to the shooting.

Onjon and Fi had insisted on developing this aspect of the place, bringing the staff more into partnership to give them a greater sense of belonging, so that they could all share in the fortunes of the project. Their wages were low but their quality of life was good and their job satisfaction high.

'Anyone can go and work on the assembly lines at Cowley,' said Onjon, 'get paid twice as much and do the work of a moron. It's their choice.'

The choice of Mr Frith, the retired postman, was to work at Rawle for nothing. When employed by the GPO he had ensured that his twice-daily deliveries to Rawle coincided with Moot where his authority as having before the war served as a footman to the Marquess of somewhere-or-other was duly respected. He came into his own on formal occasions where he would don white gloves, a tailcoat and colossal dignity. In the present circumstances there could be no paid employment for him at Rawle and hardly any grand occasions either, but for the pleasure of hearing himself say 'M'lord...m'lady,' he would turn up and perform light duties.

Having established himself as a friend to the family, Johnny too was almost a member of it, little though he had to contribute, and he felt at home there. Everyone was interested to hear how he was getting on so he shared his concern about Eaton House and its endemic petty criminality.

'They're just bored,' contributed Onjon. 'Remember all that awful learning of boring things at school – and you've got a *brain*.'

'Sounds as if they need some games,' said Lord Nidd,

Mr Frith was in favour of beating but Johnny explained that the boys could not be sent home to doting Hampstead mothers with weals on their bottoms.

' "Spare the rod and spoil the child",' persisted Mr Frith.

'Sounds as if they're spoiled in a different way already,' was Lady Nidd's contribution.

'Talking of spoiling,' said Lord Nidd, 'don't you think you're rather overdoing it with that animal, Fiona?'

Nobody had been very enthusiastic about this little black pig, an exotic, that Fi had acquired. The objection that 'Pigs belong in a sty' Fi countered with 'He's not that kind of pig. He's a pet. They'll be as popular as cats and dogs before long.'

This dubious assertion went uncontested.

'Piggy' occupied substantial personal quarters in a corner of the room. Fi had hoped he would share accommodation with the dogs beside the Aga in the kitchen but the latter had declined to take him to their bosoms, though they hadn't outright ostracised him.

'Not exactly a beaut, is he?' commented Johnny cautiously. He didn't want to offend Fi who was kneeling beside the animal and tending it, her curtains of dark hair as ever screening her face. With Fi you not only couldn't tell what she was thinking, you couldn't even see her expression. She was like her mother in thinking and feeling more than she said or showed. Any remark made to her carried a risk: how would she react?

'He's got conjunctivitis.' Fi was applying ointment from a tiny tube, at the same time scratching his back with a dry scrubbing brush.

'Shall I do the pacifying,' Johnny offered, 'while you do the doctoring?'

He wondered whether she had been listening to the conversation about his boys. Or was she entirely wrapped up in her own concerns?

Without looking up or pausing in her ministrations Fi handed him the brush. She was crouched on the floor, concentrating like a child at an absorbing game that she is not only greatly enjoying but is determined also to win. Piggy, caught between pleasure and discomfort, emitted a medley of sounds, none of them very pleasant on the ear. He was black-skinned and black-bristled and had one upward-projecting growth on the outside of his lower jaw.

'Is that a tooth or a tusk?' Johnny enquired.

Fi ignored the question and continued her application of the unguent for his eye complaint. This necessitated the use of rubber gloves, the unused one of which Piggy was munching on with a wet squeaky noise.

'He'll swallow that thing,' warned Mrs Brydon, 'if you're not careful.' She was not keen on this new denizen of the servants' hall but she knew Miss Fiona and her animals. Pet indeed! Dogs she was used to, getting under her feet in the kitchen, though her father wouldn't even have the collie in the house when she was a girl.

The dog population at Rawle had diminished in recent years, Johnny noticed. Of Lord Nidd's two black labs, Hector and Alexander, the elder, Hector, had been called to his fathers. The master's Jack Russell, Sharples, had grown out of his bounce but was still vigorous. The brown cocker spaniel who had lost an eye to a badger had been incorporated into the compost beneath the new nectarine in the walled garden. Of the two quiet and indistinguishable border terriers allied to the lady of the house one, Goofy, had turned nasty and been destroyed, while the other, Pluto, was greying in the muzzle but still going about his business. The dowager's Pekinese,

Shang and Hai, which spent their lives on their mistress's bed, had been adopted by the big house following her death but had not settled to the more robust regime there and had been given away to a hairdresser in Chipping Norton who would provide the satin bedspread life to which they considered themselves entitled by nature and previous usage.

'We worked out that the whole lot were costing more to feed than a couple of people,' explained Lord Nidd, 'and the vet's bills!' He turned to Sharples seated demurely beside his chair in hope of a small share in his master's Chocolate Digestive. 'Send you to the knackers, shall we?' In truth he would sooner send himself to the knackers, for he was a soft man in spite of his stature, his patrician stride and the tweediness of his garments – and getting softer with age.

Being taken back to the station in the old Land Rover (a hundred and forty-nine thousand miles on the clock and still going strong) Johnny remarked to Onjon that the old man seemed to be all right about the way things were going at Rawle.

'Oh, he's fine. Mum too, in her way.'

'Fi seems to be enjoying it all.'

'Very much so, don't know what I'd do without her.'

'Still doesn't say much, does she? I thought it was an adolescent thing but she's a bit old for that.'

'That's always been Fi. Doesn't talk, but thinks – and feels.'

'Does she have any sort of social life – I mean, outside Rawle? Boyfriend or anything?'

'She doesn't seem to have any interest that way. Rawle seems to be everything to her – for now, at any rate. And how's *your* love life going? The Melissa thing all over?'

Ah, yes – 'the Melissa thing'. All over indeed. Just a dull ache … what a cliché! but that was just how it felt, a hurt to which he had become so accustomed that it was simply an integral part of being who he was, like a limp.

'No one else on the scene?'

No one else. He supposed there would be. In time. But now? Oh, Melissa – how I miss ya! Oh, Melissa, how I miss ya! His heartbreak reduced to an idiotic jingle repeated a million times, a prisoner counting days that never diminished the years.

'And your folks, how are they? Enjoying the new place?'

This gave Johnny a twinge of guilt at having gone to Rawle rather than his own home at half-term. For something quite awkward was creeping up on him, namely that he now actually felt more comfortable at Rawle than he did at home with his parents. This had actually been the case for some time but only now since his year away from them in India and the family's departure from his childhood home had he become fully aware of it. A witty friend had once compared parents to a couple of old and unmatching armchairs someone had given you without first enquiring whether you wanted them; you couldn't dispose of them for fear of offending the giver so just had to make the best of them. To his parents Johnny was loving and dutiful, umbilical and unreflective. He had never rebelled or been difficult. Parents were people you didn't have to think about much: it was their job to think about you. Up to a point anyway, for they shouldn't think more about you than you thought about yourself – a tendency of mothers, he'd noticed – and start interfering or making unwelcome suggestions. They should be in the background, loving you unconditionally but unostentatiously, providing a home and a warm welcome at whatever time you chose to favour them with your presence. Money also they should provide, for while you might take a little holiday job the proceeds were entirely for optional extras like a new gramophone or a bicycle, not the fundamentals of food and clothing which it was their duty to supply.

As an only child Johnny had blithely accepted his parents' devotion, itself enhanced by the death at birth of a little girl younger than him. She had not lived long enough to acquire a name or be baptised so her parents declined to see her as having died at birth, considering her to have been stillborn and therefore without a soul. Nonetheless it was understood in the family, though the subject was never mentioned, that the name Ruth – pity – represented his parents' grief at the loss, and there was on a dim shelf in his father's study a small *pieta* with the single word 'Ruth' imprinted beneath it.

Thus while Johnny enjoyed love for two he also carried

responsibility for two. What responsibility? That he should be good rather than successful, though there was nothing wrong in success. He was always expected to do his best but not required to be the best. They also hoped, of course, that he would follow in the faith in which they had brought him up; whether he would inherit his father's vocation to the ministry of that faith was of course in God's hands, not theirs. This responsibility was in Johnny's heart rather than on his mind. In order to be able to discharge it he required two things. One was that they should make no demands of him arising out of their own needs; thus they might be allowed to be ill from time to time provided it was nothing serious. Two, that while the lively little craft of his own youth and inexperience might venture out into boisterous waters they would provide his compass bearing, indeed be his haven, if not exactly required to walk on the waters to save him lest he sink.

Now this cosy compact had taken a knock in his father's promotion and the removal of the only family home he'd known to the Midlands – a term to cast gloom over the spirits of a Surrey boy. Of course there would be a room there designated 'Johnny's room' but it was in a strange house among strange people. His parents would quickly put down new roots but he would know no one. Well, for the time being he didn't really need a home for he was part of that wandering tribe of the young who, though they had some sort of rented pad of their own somewhere, laid their heads wherever they happened to be at night, not much caring what shape the pillow was.

Johnny had reflected on Lord Nidd's suggestion that the Eaton House boys needed to play games.

'We did try that once,' said Mr Oakes when Johnny proposed football on the resumption of hostilities after half-term.

'Oh, what happened?'

'It didn't work.'

There then followed a dreary catalogue of misfortunes, mistakes and maladministration involving recalcitrant groundsmen, missing boots, absconding players and parental complaints. 'Mrs Palfreyman nearly resigned.'

'Would you mind if I have another go at it, Headmaster?'

'If you really want to.'

'No harm in trying anyway.'

'Let's hope not.'

Better start with the Local Authority – they would be responsible for public playing fields, wouldn't they? There would perhaps be one of the less scenic corners of Hampstead Heath for example, probably on a slope and with muddy goal-mouths but that wouldn't matter, they didn't need Wembley Stadium.

'Local Authority?' queried Mrs Palfreyman. The greenish hue imparted to her pale face by her eyeshade added a biliousness to her testy response. If there was any 'local authority' around here she was it. 'I suppose you could look them up in the telephone book.' She rose slowly to select the relevant volume of the four large units of the London Telephone Directory and picking it out carried it over with both hands to place it carefully on the stable-door counter with the air of one who feels she should be paid a deposit for the service. The number found, Johnny knew better than to request the use of the telephone itself, an instrument jealously guarded by Mrs Palfreyman who kept it well in the background, made calls herself rarely and received them rarely, largely on account of her unwelcoming telephone manner. Should a mother be unwise enough to ring to leave a message for her son, Mrs P. would make such a performance of getting something to write on and then drag out the taking down of the message itself that the poor woman at the other end determined she would sooner walk half a mile in the pouring rain just after she'd had her hair done to leave a written message in person than attempt to give one over the phone.

So Johnny telephoned when Mrs P. was absent. To his surprise the Local Authority turned out to be more obliging than the school secretary and Johnny was offered the use of a civic amenity not far from the school. This he eagerly and promptly inspected. It was indeed muddy and unattractive but it would do.

Next, players. A notice on the board – there were no assemblies at Eaton House – attracted numerous signatures and a time was fixed. The boys would bring their kit to school on Tuesday, stowing it in the window-seat lockers of the hall. At 3.30 Johnny would accompany the twenty-or-so players on the ten-minute walk to the field. This turned out to be a somewhat disorderly procession, sub-groups of boys taking greater possession of the highway than some motorists considered them entitled to, but they all arrived unharmed and play could commence. There had been much talk en route as to who should pick sides and how these sides would be distinguished since there were no 'colours' or 'whites' in the case. All such issues were rapidly dealt with by the boys, eager to get on with it. Johnny, proud to have remembered a whistle, had a moment of gulping panic when he realised that he had failed to remember to bring a ball. Fortunately one of the boys had one and the game could begin. Then a good time was had by all in the waning light of a late autumn afternoon. There was much running about and a great deal of shouting, there were skilful passes, courageous tackles, enterprising shots, magnificent saves and memorable goals, the final whistle bringing to a close the first triumphantly successful sporting event in the school's history.

The boys were panting, muddy and pleased as dogs.

'Thanks, Mr Clarke, that was great.'

'Can we play again on Thursday?'

'We need our own colours.'

'And our own team. We could play the Hall. Bet we could beat them.'

'Who wants to come for practice on Saturday?'

And the mothers having turned up in cars as arranged to collect their children, there was parental approval too.

'Thank you so much, Mr Clarke, Alex has talked about nothing else for days. They've obviously had a wonderful time.'

Johnny returned alone in the dusk to Eaton House, aglow with satisfaction.

Still aglow with satisfaction he took this triumph to Rawle the following weekend, eager to share news of his success. But Rawle had other things on its mind, for a quantity of timber had arrived for the making of the market stalls that were to be set up in the unappealing corrugated-asbestos barn on the home farm. So the weekend was all hammers and nails and excitement. At least until it was time for him to go home. Fi it was who drove him to the station. With her natural taciturnity and the noise of the old Land Rover Johnny was not expecting much conversation. He was too tired to initiate the small talk he knew she didn't like and he was blowed if he was going to bring up the matter of his sporting triumph if no one else was interested enough to give him the opportunity. But to his surprise Fi did.

Looking ahead as she drove and as ever screened by her hair she had no awkward eye contact to make when she asked, out of the blue, in a rather deliberate tone, 'How are your boys?' And that enabled Johnny to tell someone at any rate of his success, even if Fi had little to offer by way of further enquiry or congratulation, as if she'd shot her bolt with her initial question. Perhaps, Johnny reflected pleasantly on the train to London, it had cost her quite a lot to ask it in the first place.

From time to time any school will admit a child who turns out to be a disaster.

Eaton House didn't much go in for foreigners, just the occasional diplomat's son. Angel Rodriguez, the son of a Spanish attaché of some sort, was one such.

'You'd better look after this one, Clarke,' said Mr Oakes. 'He's got virtually no English.'

'How can I teach him if he doesn't speak English?'

'You teach him to. Come on, you've taught foreigners before.'

'Yes, but…'

Angel was not Johnny's idea of Spanish, being fair-skinned and fair-haired with a roundish face radiating good-natured incomprehension. As to his command of English, Mr Oakes had not been exaggerating. All he seemed to manage was 'pe-lease' and 'thenk you.'

'So at least he can mind his p's and q's,' commented Mr Long drily.

'I can't think why we've got him,' said Johnny.

'Can't you?' Mr Long almost sneered, and rubbed his finger and thumb together in an unpleasant manner.

'Actually he's not bad at maths,' was Mr Paget's comment. 'Numbers talk to him.'

'I wish I could,' said Johnny. 'Pity he can't do maths all the time.'

Before meeting him Johnny had hoped that having a Spanish boy in his history class would lend a new perspective to their coverage of the Spanish Armada but such hopes were quickly dashed. For one thing he was not Spanish, only Spanish-speaking, being Venezuelan, while, for another, he had no understanding of the proceedings. Angel's saving grace, however, apart from his maths, was that he was a terrific colourer-in. His pencil case, actually a tin about a yard long and of an expensive Swiss make, offered a staggeringly wide range with at least half a dozen tones of a single colour, each with exotic names, as aquamarine, sky, Prussian, sapphire, like a set of gems. Johnny started him off on a rather childish colouring-in book depicting costume through the ages which Angel completed in a trice but Johnny then found a text book even more ancient than the prescribed volume in use which featured small but elaborately detailed black-and-white pictures that included battle scenes and other engaging acts of violence such as beheadings. On this Angel fell with manic intensity and was happy for hours, the resulting works of art being cut out and gummed to coloured paper for display on the back wall where Mr Oakes would be less likely to see them.

It was not only in this way that Angel brought colour to the life of Eaton House. Perhaps because of his linguistic limitations he tended to be rather mischievous and physical. Punching and pushing is a natural ingredient of normal communication between twelve-year-old boys but Angel, rumbustious in his frustration, sometimes went too far and landed another boy on the floor. The tellings-off he received for this he understood just as well as dogs understand verbal rebukes but they made no difference to his behaviour though his charade of apology over each incident was elaborate and sincere. He was popular with the other boys for where others feared to tread Angel was sure to rush in and where Angel rushed in there were sure to be lively doings.

At no time more lively than during the conker season. Playing conkers was permitted at Eaton House but strictly only outside and among the 'fresh air fiends' who had exchanged smoking for this innocent, though to Mr Feast troublesome, pastime. Angel was not of this select society and therefore not eligible to play. His active soul, pined, however, at his exclusion. He sought to gatecrash his way into this privilege by arriving at school one Monday morning with a cardboard box so large he could scarcely get it through the door. It was owing to its weight and the weakness of its bottom that it suddenly collapsed on itself and spilled its lustrous contents on to the brown lino of the hall floor, the conkers bouncing and rolling in all directions, much to the delight of the other boys who fell on them, or in some cases fell over them, to the even greater delight of the onlookers as they busily stuffed their pockets with the treasures that spilled from Angel's fructucopia and proceeded to put them to their customary purpose. Responsibility for the ensuing chaos of din and flying fragments of conkers was laid firmly at Angel's door and stern if uncomprehended words were had with him.

With this handicap of language and a propensity to trouble-making Angel's future at Eaton House could not be promising, however appreciative the father of his son's progress and however promptly he paid the fees. The feeling in the staff room was that Angel would more likely go out with a bang than a whimper.

That had been September. Things had since quietened down in Angel's vicinity apart from occasional outbursts and there was even a slight improvement in the boy's English.

Now November.

'I've received a complaint, Headmaster,' reported Mrs Palfreyman after school one dark afternoon.

'Not that Mrs Corner again, I trust,' Mr Oakes replied wearily. He'd had a lot of trouble with her. Really, modern parents, the way they interfered, why couldn't they just leave it to the school to –

'No, it's not a parent, Headmaster.' Mrs P's wandering eye was searching the horizon in perplexity. 'It's a member of the public.'

'The public' was clearly a tribe of dubious customs to be held even more firmly at arm's length than parents. Their rights were nil.

'Well, what's the complaint?'

'The woman, a Mrs Box, says that the boys have been rude and also, she thinks, thrown things at her.'

'What sort of things? And what have they said? In what way have they been rude?' Normally Mr Oakes held no brief for his pupils but if a mere member of the public were a plaintiff in a case against them he would rout such a suitor out of court.

'She wasn't very specific. It was not much more than "noises" and "things".'

Mr Oakes snorted. There was almost certainly nothing to this, a silly old body's imagination.

'Tell her to put her complaint in writing. Tell her we'll look into it.' And that would be that, thought Mr Oakes.

But it wasn't for the 'silly old body' turned out to be a perfectly sensible woman of middle years who declined to write in and firmly requested audience instead. It did seem a bit vague, she admitted, but there was definitely a sense of 'things coming at her' from Eaton House. She passed that way regularly at around lunchtime on her way back from her morning's typing at the council offices and she had experienced it more than once.

Mr Oakes was mildly unnerved by this account. The woman was far from hysterical or malicious, indeed on the contrary she seemed almost apologetic and he felt there was some uncomfortable truth in it. What could he do? While he was pondering the matter another complaint was lodged, this time in more forceful manner by a youngish man in painter's overalls who banged loudly on the door to denounce the 'bloody little hooligans' of Eaton House, and stomped off.

'Clarke, you'd better look into this,' declared Mr Oakes as one too busy and important for such petty police work. 'See what you can find out.'

Johnny did not feel he was training for a career in education by such activity but had little choice in the matter.

'Well, Headmaster, I think we should begin by talking to the fresh air boys – that's obviously where the trouble's coming from.'

'Talking's a waste of time.'

'Well, at least it'll give them a chance to bring a stop to this of their own accord.'

This seemed to Johnny a much more educational way of dealing with the matter.

'Very well,' agreed Mr Oakes reluctantly, 'if that doesn't work the place is out of bounds.'

And it didn't work. The typist woman, Mrs Box, complained again, this time rather angrily and hinting that her employment with the council placed her rather well for having the matter officially investigated. She didn't want to take such a step but…

And so an edict went out that henceforth 'the front' was out of bounds, regrettable though it might be to deprive the boys of their little escape outdoors.

As this measure had the effect of making the hall even more crowded and noisy during the lunch hour Johnny took it upon himself to allow the fresh air boys to use his classroom as a little common room of their own. He was pleased to see that Angel had been adopted by them and thus removed from the mainstream of recreation so that the incessant games of round the table could proceed without that extra element of Spanish expletives and the throwing of bats that Angel, who was intensely competitive, brought to the game. Though Johnny was of course responsible for the boys at that time and in that place he would not be supervising them; indeed he allowed them to have the door closed which was not normally permitted, and also gave them to understand that he would not be coming in on them unannounced. He was pleased that his philosophy of 'treat them like adults and they'll behave like adults' was borne out by results for things were surprisingly quiet considering Angel was of the party. This was perhaps explained by their having some sort of game to play that involved warlike figures of which Angel possessed many. They were the current craze and none was crazier than Angel. Mr Oakes had not been in favour of this arrangement of Johnny's, particularly as regards the closed door aspect, but as it brought some much valued quiet to the otherwise rather raucous Eaton House lunch hour he let it be. So Johnny felt vindicated.

Except that the problems didn't stop. More complaints were received and Johnny was faced with the incriminating fact that these alleged assaults were all perpetrated during the lunch hour, the only time the boys were free to make trouble. But how could they, now that they were banned from 'the front'? The back quarters of the St Botolphs premises occupied by Eaton House had windows only to the south and west when the complaints were received from people passing down Eaton Drive, to the north. And yet – no, wait a minute – heavens! He'd forgotten the window in his own classroom, the window whose broken cord Mr Paget had mended so that it could be opened. But surely that was too high up. And then suddenly there returned to him the remark made by Bet, the cleaner, only the other day: 'Why do they need to go walking all over the desks, I wonder,' a remark which Johnny attributed to Bet's characteristically hyperbolical manner of speech, for with her anything that had to be done more than once had to be done 'a thousand times', a small collection of litter was 'a great mound of rubbish' and so on. So Johnny thought little of it and explained to Bet that the boys had some game going that perhaps created a bit of a mess on the desk tops. But now the remark came back to him with a sudden draining of the blood from his heart (at least that was what it felt like) and he realised what must be happening. The boys, probably inspired by the mischievous Angel, were clambering on to a desk in order to be able to hurl abuse or small objects or whatever it was from the window at the passers-by.

So that was it. They had taken advantage of the privacy they had been given (against Mr Oakes' better judgment) to misbehave and bring the establishment into disrepute. Well, he'd soon put a stop to that! No more trust, no more privilege.

But wait, did he really want to see 'I told you so' written all over his headmaster's face? Did he really want to be held responsible for this disgrace, to see that superior expression of Mr Long's that said, 'Gullible youngster, trusting fool'? No, he couldn't face that and – heavens! – there might have to be expulsions if this came out. No, there was another way. If the window had been unopenable when he arrived it could now be returned to that state. He would remove the cord so that even standing on a desk the boys would be unable to reach the catch at the top and open the window. Ha ha! That would fix them. Then there would at last be an end to these problems for, deprived of the side window as well as the front, there was absolutely no way in which the boys could continue their antisocial behaviour. Johnny himself should get some credit for having relieved his headmaster of this disciplinary burden and peace could be restored.

He could hardly suppress a smile when next day one of the privileged lunchtime boys appealed for the restoration of the window-opening facility, citing the improbable stuffiness of the room. So that was that.

But it wasn't. Complaints continued. Mr Oakes was becoming deeply restive. Johnny was at his wits' end. Mrs Box was the most articulate of the several aggrieved passers-by. Johnny got from her a more precise picture of what the offensiveness emanating from the establishment actually consisted of beyond the hitherto alleged 'noises' and 'things'. What exactly were they? Obscenities? Apple cores? Bits of old conker perhaps? Stones? It was hard to say – Mrs Box was trying to be helpful – but the noises were not words you could recognise as such, they were almost animal noises or perhaps words in a foreign language (aha!) 'and these noises,' Mrs Box went on, 'they hurt, they sting.' No, she didn't mean the words were hurtful as such but that they physically hurt, sometimes anyway as if the words, the sounds, were accompanied by sharp little stones or something though she'd never actually seen anything that it could be.

For lack of any more positive lead Johnny went out into Eaton Drive to see the situation from the victim's point of view.

There loomed the bulk of the church, tall stained glass windows in the nave, sort of arrow-slit apertures to the lower-roofed side aisle bit, as he supposed it (Johnny had never actually been inside the church), and there was the blank brick expanse of the Eaton House part of the premises, with the stone steps leading up to the gothic front door. And there – yes – there was the window of his classroom, quite high up, the only – wait a minute, what was that? Another window, this one with obscure diamond-leaded panes, set further up, smaller and off to one side in the middle of the gable end. But what could that be? There was no other floor to the building, no storey above them, so how come there was a window? What did it look out of? An attic perhaps. Well, whatever it was, it wouldn't be accessible to any of the boys who were absolutely confined to their very limited premises, every square foot of which was plain to see. There were no nooks and crannies, no narrow backstairs leading upwards from dim corners.

Johnny was stumped.

Then it was Bet again. 'Walking on the desks is one thing,' she complained to Johnny, 'walking on the walls is another.'

'Walking on the walls?'

'What do you call that then?' Bet pointed a broom handle in the direction of some black marks high on the wall right above the master's desk. It was as if something had been struck against the wall but in a sweeping or swinging rather than a hammering motion. There were several such marks if not in the same place at least in the same area. What could cause that? And so high up? A scuff on a skirting board was one thing but these marks, so strong and above head height?

'Them's shoes,' remarked Bet with all the glum authority of one who has spent a lifetime removing every kind of stain, blemish, patch or smear from every conceivable surface. 'Rubber-soled shoes.'

The best Johnny could think of was that the boys had invented some sort of game that involved hurling footwear at some target on the wall. It didn't seem very probable but there was no knowing what children could invent and he didn't actually know what they got up to in there. From their clambering on desks to make rude noises at passers-by through the window it was clear that this game of soldiers they were ostensibly absorbed in was just a front for more mischievous activities. Chucking shoes at the wall indeed!

And then he looked up at the ceiling – was that streaked as well? No, but – oy,oy! – what was that in the ceiling immediately above the desk? The frame of an opening, an unobtrusive wooden square of no more than eighteen inches painted in the same white as the ceiling but looking grubby – fingerprint grubby, in fact.

'That'll be the way to the loft,' said Bet.

Ah.

They were heavy, these old desks with the lift-up lids and thick wooden runners but this was not an operation in which he could call for assistance. Clearing his own desk and emptying the boy's desk nearest it, Johnny managed to heave the one upon the other. Shoving aside his fear of heights he made himself clamber awkwardly on top, carefully not looking down, to find he had to bend his head slightly to keep clear of the ceiling so that he could easily apply upward pressure with his fingers to the loft trap and flip it open. Rising slightly on his toes, he was able to peer over the rim into the space revealed. It was of course dark but there, at the end, was the little window with the diamond-leaded panes which admitted a dull yellow glow from the streetlight outside.

Now to get bodily in. A reach and a heave should do it with a bit of awkward dangling in the process. Ah! that's how the shoe marks on the wall came about. (But don't look down!) Once securely in and panting somewhat from nerves as well as exertion, Johnny crouched to get used to his surroundings. Light from below now adding to light from the little window was enough to make out what was what. Well, well, so this was it! A nice little nest they'd made up here! Peering and groping in the dimness, Johnny came across a torch. That was handy. He flashed its beam around but not very searchingly: there were too many sloping roofs and dim corners and spaces of darkness stretching away in several directions for comfort. Any sort of unpleasant things might lie there : it wasn't just heights he was afraid of. But he noticed something on the wall just to the left of the little window. It was a paper target hanging on a nail, blue, white and red concentric rings, a used target, for it had holes in it. The boys had turned the place into a shooting range! Surely not. They'd never get a gun past the authorities and up here.

Now what else was there? A lightweight aluminium ladder; that must have been up here already surely. A large squat candle and a box of matches – crikey, the fire risk! – but no cigarettes; a Harrogate Toffee tin containing boiled sweets – bullseyes, in fact, (ha ha); another small round tin, heavy, rattly – yes, air-gun pellets ; and finally, folded into the rug – aha! – the weapon itself, not a rifle, but a pistol. Webley .177, it said. So that's where Markwell's stolen gun had disappeared to.

Got them! The boys, deprived of their original site outside, had switched to using the window in the classroom so obligingly provided by his own foolish trustingness. Deprived of that, they had gone into the roof and continued their strange shouting and shooting through the missing panes of the highest window in the building. The crafty little blighters! Who would have thought that boys so dim could be so resourceful? And of course that explained Mrs Box's remark about being 'stung' by the words thrown at her from the building: the stings were the pellets of the air-gun. From such a weapon there was no bang to alert the victim to – it was just a release of compressed air – she would simply be aware, if at all, of something small and hard hitting her clothes or her skin. She wouldn't know what it was unless she happened to look down and see the little grey slug. Dangerous? He thought not. The pistol, though definitely more of a real weapon than a toy, was surely not powerful enough to do damage or inflict real hurt. But if it hit someone in the eye?

The cold rush swept again through Johnny's heart. Because of his stupid indulgence of the boys in allowing them to have their private place he had in effect set them up in a criminal activity. Oh yes – criminal, for what they were doing was no less than that. When one of those passers-by actually discovered she was being shot at it would be a police matter and hell to pay for the individual boys concerned as well as the school itself. Why, if it got into the press that could be the end of the place. There was no time to lose.

Johnny realised that he must tell his headmaster. Although the investigation of this offence had been delegated to him his enquiries were now complete. All the evidence was to hand and it only remained for Mr Oakes, with the weight of his headmagisterial authority, to confront the culprits and mete out due punishment, having in mind of course the importance of hushing it up. But do I really want to get him involved? wondered Johnny. Surely better to deal with the matter myself. I know exactly the nature of the case and who the culprits are. I will confront them, make them aware of the gravity of their offence and shut the whole thing down quietly. That's the prime requirement – to put a stop to it. Mr Oakes doesn't want the truth, he wants peace, and I will give it him. There would be no need for any blame or punishment or furore of any kind.

So the next day Johnny went into action. Catching them red-handed was too much to hope for but nonetheless he was slightly disappointed, on entering his classroom during the next lunch hour, to find the half dozen regulars clustered round a pair of desks on which the curious creatures of their war games were set out. They looked up in surprise since he had never come in before, having assured them of their privacy. There was no sudden scuffling for innocent positions, no sense of any nefariousness interrupted, leave alone a desk incriminatingly stood on his desk or dangling legs scuffing the wall.

'I want your attention, boys. Now this is just between you and me. It won't go any further but it is a serious matter so in return I need you to be truthful, to be absolutely honest with me.'

The boys looked a little baffled, but then in their experience masters were occasionally liable to take this sort of serious line and it wasn't always clear why they did; better pay attention, though.

'Right, which of you has been up in the loft?'

No one answered but Johnny could tell he was indeed on to something. He jerked an accusing thumb in the direction of the incriminating shoe marks on the wall behind him.

'Well?'

No answer, but some shifty looks.

'Bowers, have you been up in the loft?'

'Sort of, sir.'

'What do you mean, sort of? Either you –'

'What he means, I think, sir,' offered Zuckerman, 'is that he's looked up there.' He paused. 'We all have.' There was no dissent from this general confession.

'Oh, just a look, was it? None of you has actually set foot inside the loft?'

Johnny was suddenly cross. He had generously appealed for trust and been repaid with evasion.

'Right, well let's all get a proper look up there, shall we, and then we shall see exactly what we shall see when we're all up inside there together. Angel, Francis, put that desk on top of –'

Suddenly there were tears from Davidson.

'I can't, sir. Must I? I'm frightened.'

Oh, here was a good act! All right to fire air-guns at old ladies but suddenly we're afraid of the dark. Ha!

'He's afraid of rats, sir,' put in Francis.

'Yes, sir, there are rats up there, we hear them. We did have a look, I admit, sir, we all did but none of us went right in, it's horrible up there, all dark and dusty and horrible and none of us went *right* in.'

'I wouldn't even look,' said the plaintive Davidson.

'I wouldn't go up there on my own for a hundred pounds.'

'I wouldn't go for a thousand!'

This sudden eruption of candour, the simple expression of boyish feeling in boyish language and most of all the unashamed admission of fear stopped Johnny in his tracks. He couldn't force them up there. But he couldn't leave it that, either.

'All right, whose is the air pistol?'

No answer.

'Well it must belong to one of you, so whose is it?'

All-round incomprehension .

'If no one owns up to this I'm turning the whole thing over to the headmaster and then you'll really be –'

But what was that outside in the hall? 'Anyone seen Mr Clarke?' It was Mr Oakes, loud, urgent.

Johnny opened the door.

'I'm here, Headmaster. There's something I need to tell you if you would –'

'And there's something I need to tell *you*. Come with me please.'

Once inside the staff room he turned on Johnny.

'Another complaint, Clarke, and this time it's urgent. Your enquiries are running out of time.' He held out his hand. 'Do you know what this is?'

Something suddenly flicked inside Johnny's mind.

'Has the complaint been made today?' he asked. 'I mean of something that *happened* today?'

'Yes, just now.'

'Just now? This lunch hour?'

'Yes, I tell you – this very minute. The woman came straight in, immediately it happened. I said, Do you know what this is?'

In the palm of Mr Oakes's hand lay a gravel-sized grey metallic object.

'Yes, I know what it is,' Johnny replied, 'it's an air-gun pellet. Headmaster, excuse me, I must –'

And he was out of the room in a flash and back to his classroom. The boys were still there bemused, uncertain.

'Right, out, all of you. Quickly now. And don't come back in. (You silly innocents, you!) Francis, give me a hand with this desk – quickly – and quietly… I said out, the rest of you… that's it, thank you, Francis, now you go out too and don't let anyone in.'

'Not even the headmaster, sir?'

'Especially not the headmaster. Now out you go and shut the door.'

'I don't know if I'll be able to –'

'OUT!'

Johnny clambered up on to the desk. Mustn't hurry and make a mess of it. Mustn't waste any time though, either. Standing cautiously upright and flexing his fingers, Johnny prepared for action, giving himself a few seconds to recover his breath for the next, the crucial move. Then he raised his arms and with a swift upward shove threw open the trap door.

Daylight this time, more than enough to make out what barely a minute before he had suddenly realised he was going to see: the ferrety face, little eyes gleaming in the dark.

'Ah!' he said, 'got any bullseyes today, Mr Feast? Who'd have thought you liked boiled sweets!'

3

TALBOT COLLEGE 2

This was of course too long a tale for Johnny to tell to the headmaster of Talbot College, even without the aftermath: his pride in single-handedly exonerating the boys of Eaton House – particularly the innocent Angel – from the charge of assaulting innocent passers-by, in solving the mystery of Markwell's missing air pistol as well, quite possibly, as other thefts from the Eaton House premises. And it would be too long to tell how Mr Oakes used his knowledge of the larcenous Mr Feast's iniquities to subdue him utterly – there would be no more trouble from the verger of St Botolphs!

So what had Johnny learned from his time at Eaton House? Not much. Then what had he given? Well, was it just his imagination or did his dramatic uncovering of the worm in the St Botolphs apple lighten the whole atmosphere at Eaton House? And didn't the expectation of Christmas seem, in spite of December's dwindling days, like the prospect of a sunnier life for all? When he left at the end of term they all made a nice fuss of him. 'You've brightened the place up,' smiled Mr Paget.

But the headmaster's question had been: How is a school to reconcile the IFI – the Implicit Fees Imperative – with the requirement for true education, with the importance of sending children out into the world not just with exam certificates but with a love of learning? So could any part of Johnny's experience at Eaton House answer him? Had any real education taken place there or was it just the grind of memorisation and the treadmill of practice exam papers? Would Mr Long's mean-minded severity imbue any boy with an interest in foreign languages? Would Mr Paget's bumbling explanations open any boy's eyes to the intriguing logic of algebra? Probably not, though it had to be said of both teachers that their pupils did actually learn something – albeit in Mr Paget's case less about algebra than about plumbing and welding.

Still comfortable in his armchair, the headmaster had exchanged one yellow-socked ankle for the other and his pipe was out. The dog was still on Johnny's feet with every appearance of content.

'Actually,' said Johnny, 'the best thing was the Battle of Bosworth Field on the ping-pong table. Mr Oakes had an astonishing collection of toy soldiers and he'd painted a cloth with the geographical features of the battlefield, with a rise here and a marsh there, and he had the different forces in their places: Northumberland's, Henry's, Richard's of course and Stanley's two bodies off to the side. And he explained what happened. He had a long stick with a little blade on it like pretty ATS girls use in the ops room in war films and he moved the soldiers around to show how the battle developed. Sometimes he got the boys to do the moving. You should have seen their faces! They were riveted. There wouldn't have been a boy leaving school that day who didn't have a good knowledge of that great historical event and hungry for more where that came from. I said to the headmaster, "Why don't we get the film of Olivier in *Richard III*, then we'd be doing English as well?" But of course we hadn't got a projector. "Well, what about a visit to Bosworth Field itself?" I suggested, "it's just up the A5 in the Midlands somewhere, we could do it in a day trip, maybe throw in a bit of geography at the same time?" '

'And how did he respond to that?' queried the headmaster with a smile as if he knew the answer.

'He said they couldn't afford the time out of class with that term's C.E. looming. "The parents aren't paying for outings and besides they don't like extras on the bill. Their fees they pay in sadness and –" '

' "their extras they pay in anger." He was quite right about that,' agreed the headmaster, laughing. 'And was he wrong, do you think, to take that line?'

'Not wrong, exactly but –'

'But you're a young man just starting out and a bit of excitement, a bit of adventure, is more to your taste than keeping dull parents happy and pushing reluctant children through exams.'

'It's just – I want to make learning more interesting for my pupils than it was for me.'

'So I should think and that's a good motivation. Now did your spell in the state sector give you the opportunity for such adventure? I hear there are some exciting innovations in the new comprehensives.' He spoke as of the rumoured activities of distant tribes without the law.

Johnny's first encounter with the state sector had been at a primary school in Walthamstow. The Barrow Rd First School was a far cry from his own prep school. The children, who wore no uniform, seemed to be tiny and astonishingly loud: how could they hear one another at their games if they were all screaming at the same time? And there were hundreds of them zooming round the playground with random violence but astonishingly no accident. What were they doing? And how on earth could he cope with a classroom full of deafening midgets? 'All right, children, sit down please. Now what we're going to do today is…' But by the time he got to them they were already seated, not in rows but in groups of four and under the headmistress's direction were all working quietly away so there was no need of the 'Sit down, children' approach.

'Know how to work a tape recorder?' the headmistress asked.

'No. I'd probably break it. I know how to work a gramophone.'

'Better stick to the radio.'

Good heavens ! What on earth was a wireless to do with teaching? Well, it was music, 'Casey Jones with a hammer in his hand.' The children were equipped with triangles and other instruments Johnny didn't recognise as such, tubes and whistles and things. Luckily one of the women teachers was on hand to help and play the piano. By the time Casey Jones was somehow despatched 'to the promised land' ('with his hammer in his hand') Johnny was pink with relief and wondering which was worse – struggling on his own or being an incapable spare man on the sidelines.

But he got other help, small children willing to give patient assistance to floundering adults. Little Maria, the Maltese girl with pigtails and the pebble glasses that magnified the pupils to soul-searching proportions, guided Johnny through his fumbling efforts to manage the class. 'We'll need our reading books now… Mrs Kershaw will give us some more chalk… the paintbrushes go back in this cupboard… ' It was as if her strained eyesight were due to excessive study in dim conditions like some poor medieval scholar and her enlarged gaze bent on Johnny made him feel dreadfully exposed in his ignorance and incapability. To his astonishment the little things mostly just got on with it, collecting the next work card, lending each other pencil sharpeners, hardly needing Johnny except to ask to 'go to the toilet please, Miss – Sir.' The headmistress looked in from time to time and went quietly around calming an anxiety here, demonstrating a pencil stroke there before withdrawing again, leaving the world a better place. Johnny thought there could be nothing finer than to be like her, combining professional expertise with private virtue, a gifted teacher, a capable administrator and a good woman.

But Outram Park was something else.

4

OUTRAM PARK

O victory forget your underwear we're free.
(Allen Ginsberg: *Howl.*)

'Eddy – Eddy Two Shoes we called him,' said Val. 'Mr Eddington his real name.'

'Why Two Shoes?' asked Johnny.

'He had two pairs of shoes. The father of one of the boys was a cobbler and when Eddy was walking between one school site and another this man would catch him up in the street with the one pair of shoes Eddy wasn't wearing and which he had mended. Eddy would stop right there and lean on whatever child he was walking with, because he was never on his own, Eddy, always with a child or a parent or a teacher or maybe just some local he knew, he would take off the shoes and hand them over to this cobbler father in exchange for the mended ones which would be polished as well as repaired. The cobbler would look at the pair that needed resoling, tut-tutting at their condition like a parent with a toddler that's got its clothes dirty – you know, pretending to be disapproving but actually loving it. Eddy had saved his boy from being sent to Borstal somehow or other and this father would have died for him if there'd been the call for it, which there nearly was once but that's another story. Then with his mended shoes on Eddy would get out his wallet – he was always spraying money around – and say, 'Eight and six, I think, Mr Stylianou,' and Mr Stylianou, he was a Cypriot, his English wasn't very good, he'd say, 'Bugger the money. You give me money I hit you.' And there'd almost be a fight because Eddy was determined to pay and he always got his way in everything. Once Eddy said when Mr Stylianou wouldn't take the money, "All right I'll leave it here," and he put it down on the pavement and walked away.'

'So what happened to the money?'

'The kid he was with picked it up, I think.'

Johnny liked to get Val talking. For one thing he found something very soothing in her slight northern accent and for another it gave him a break from her relentless lovemaking. She'd been put in charge of him when he arrived at Outram Park Comprehensive as a supply teacher. 'Supply teachers normally don't know their arses from their elbows,' she'd said encouragingly and looking at Johnny as if he would definitely fall into that category. 'They're either too strict and don't last a week or let the kids do what they like and don't last a fortnight. How long are you supposed to be here for?'

'A term.'

'Christ Almighty!'

Anyway she initiated Johnny into Outram Park, the two sites separated by half a mile so that you were usually fifteen minutes late for the lesson at the other place by which time the kids had created mayhem in the classroom unless the head over there – there were two heads, one on each site, who were supposed to work in partnership, ha ha – unless she, Mrs Boardman, had come by and settled them down, 'down' being the operative word with Ma Boardman who ate nails. So two sites – split site, split personality – a six-day curricular week so that it was never simply Monday or Thursday but Day 1 or Day 4, and you had a job to remember.

'And what have you done,' Johnny asked Val, 'to get landed with me?'

'I'm young, I suppose. Oh, and to integrate me with the other staff. One of Half-Baker's ideas.' Mr Baker was Ma Boardman's fellow head.

'And Half-Baker,' Val explained, 'because his ideas are –'

'Yes, I get it,' said Johnny. 'Why do you need integrating anyway?'

'Because I'm a one-woman department.'

'And what department is that?'

'The remedial department. Eight hundred kids, four hundred need remedial attention, all they've got is me. Do I look overworked?'

She waved her fag around. Overworked or not, she looked damn good to Johnny – large, luscious, with wild thick brown hair, miniskirt…

'And what exactly are you remedying?' he asked.

'Heard of dyslexia?'

'Dys…?'

'…lexia. Know what it is?'

'Well, 'dys' as in 'no good', 'lexia' as in 'reading', so dyslexia is squiffy reading. Is that right?'

Val was looking at him. 'Ooh! Classically educated, I see,' she said in a mock-posh accent.

'But we teach them to read in the English department – or try to.'

'Dyslexia's different,' Val explained. 'It's like being colour-blind. It's the way you see things.'

'How do I diagnose it?'

'In writing there's a tendency to compose words phonetically, so 'c-o-m-e' would be 'c-u-m', 'a-l-l' would be 'o-r-l'. And they get b's and d's confused.'

'Ah yes, I remember a boy like that at my prep school. Bennet his name was. The headmaster called him Nebbet. '

'That must have been good for his confidence.'

'My prep school didn't go in for confidence.'

'You don't seem short of it.'

'Just an act.'

Confidence was what Johnny's head of department, Norman Brewster, certainly had. Real confidence. His name was misleading, suggesting a lower-middle class roundness if not stolidity, when its bearer was actually small and neat and almost sharp in appearance, if not manner. 'The Norm' they called him as he went about his business, whether it was patrolling a corridor on duty, playing bridge in the staff room or teaching, with dainty but not effeminate imperturbability and economy of movement, voice and expression. Sitting in on his lesson –

Val had persuaded Half-Baker that some observation before going solo might give the supply teachers a better chance of survival, like Spitfire pilots – Johnny noted a man of almost dandified presentation. He wore a pinstripe suit of a unique reddish-brown colour together with grey shoes neat as a ballerina's. This, not exactly Savile Row in taste perhaps but faultless in the wearing, was his unvarying uniform, underneath it a white shirt with dark pink tie and matching handkerchief in his top pocket, often a flower in his buttonhole.

With his large class (that Johnny was due to take over) he was reading a novel apparently about the gentler aspects of beekeeping in pre-war rural France – an odd choice for a group mostly composed of Jamaican teenagers bigger than he was but the pleasant calm of a warm summer afternoon in the Languedoc pervaded the lesson, the boys taking it in turn to read, some of them haltingly but there was no sniggering, so that Johnny wondered what the fuss was about and why he needed to waste time on this observation business.

Until he came to take the class himself.

Johnny thought that though the Eaton House teaching was of course a piece of cake he had had the previous experience of facing up to a mixed class of fifty Indian students with little inclination to learn and less English to learn with. That had been the crucible of his initiation, the lion's den from which he had eventually and not without some mauling emerged victorious or at any rate alive. So with that to his credit this lot, a mere thirty-five or so and mostly native English speakers, was bound to be a walkover, wasn't it?

No, it wasn't. All over again it was like taking the tiller from an expert helmsman when you yourself have no experience of the role. Still, you've watched, you've seen how it works, the basic principles are evident – it can't be too difficult. 'Just hold her steady, make for that point.' Simple. You grasp the tiller, warm and smooth with manly usage to which you are now yourself contributing, and for a little while it is easy, gratifying, you feel the gentle firmness of the water in partnership with the guiding blade in your hand, natural power and human governance working together to drive the boat on, your aim and your course are true. ('That's it, Odibayo, well read. Who's next? Go on, Hopkins, I think this next paragraph could tell us something we don't know...Well, maybe, Thomas, but let's just read it first, shall we?') Then you notice a slight drift in the direction of the prow so you apply a little corrective pressure. ('No, from the top of the page, Hopkins, we've read that bit.') But nothing happens. A little more pressure, because the prow has obstinately veered further off-course regardless of your action. ('Don't laugh, anyone can make that kind of mistake.') Still no response. Is it a factor of the wind that will self-correct without further intervention on your part? Some hope. The boat is now plainly headed in quite the wrong direction. ('He can't read if you distract him – leave him to concentrate.') You begin to panic and positively shove the tiller away from you – ignore that if you can! ('Hopkins is reading, there's no need for anyone else to say anything. So, silence, please. Go on, Hopkins.') But it's too late, the boat has turned too far into the wind, the mainsail is slacking, the jib is flapping and any moment now you will have involuntarily gone about without having done any of those tricky things with ropes necessary to get on to the opposite tack. Suddenly the boat is drifting, sails are rioting ('Get down from there, you...what's your name? I said what's – and you, both of you, down!') loose ropes are rattling and tangling ('Everyone, back to your places – *now*!') and you are completely out of control. Only an experienced helmsman can get you back. They are literally climbing up the walls to look out of the windows set so high but not high enough but then, the bell must have gone, they're streaming out of the door, leaving you and your pitiful craft hopelessly grounded if not actually splintered on the rocks. You have omitted to take the books in so you'll have to collect them yourself, one by one. Some are still open, that one's clearly just been scrawled in but you can't now tell by whom, some are on the floor and this one's spine's gone in the mêlée. It'll take you the whole of break. *And* you have forgotten to set homework.

The Norm puts the whole class in detention and takes it himself. Johnny feels that it should be he who is detained.

'There is corporal punishment, you know,' Val tells him.

'Official or unofficial?'

'Both.'

'I felt like hitting them.'

'Don't. If you're angry you could get it wrong. Anyway you don't seem to me to be a corporal punishment sort of person.'

'I'm not. So what should I do?'

'Apart from learning all their names for a start and not letting them go until you've finished your business, you mean?'

'Yes, apart from that.'

'Send one or two to Half-Baker.'

'Who will do what?'

'Give them a half-baked talking-to and a half-baked punishment.'

'What's the good of that?'

'It'll slow them up.'

'I don't want slow pupils.'

'You don't want to be stampeded in the rush though either.'

'True.'

Chalky White has a different view.

'You are the ruler so you have a ruler. A ruler has a flat side for sound effect and low-to-medium impact on bare flesh. Avoid the face. Aim for the hands. The ruler also has an edge for medium-to-high impact. Target any part of the human frame, again avoiding the face, though neck and head can be recommended to the experienced. Remember that the edge, if applied skilfully, can have effect through clothing, even a blazer. Avoid the hands – you might misfire and incapacitate a writing finger, you might leave a mark. Best not to leave marks.'

'You've always used a ruler?'

'For the first twenty years or so I did. Haven't for a long time. Now I use Beaky.'

'Beaky?'

'Come to my classroom – I'll show you…Oh! you still here, Danny? I said twenty minutes and here you are after thirty. I'd forgotten you. Now I want you to introduce Beaky to Mr Clarke. I can't see him, Danny. You haven't lost him, have you? Ah! but what are you doing hiding him away in your desk? He's supposed to be sitting in the inkwell – you know that – keeping an eye on you and telling the world what a naughty boy you've been. I think we'd better make that twenty minutes into forty, don't you, Beaky? Come here – what's that you say? Definitely forty, I knew you'd agree with me. Now some people, Mr Clarke, think that Beaky is just a wooden spoon painted to look like an angry old schoolmaster. See those red cheeks! Look at that mortarboard, almost falling off his head he's in such a rage. Now why is he angry, Danny?'

'The boys and girls aren't working, sir.'

'Is that all?'

'Someone's talking, sir.'

'And when does he get angriest, Danny?'

'Someone hasn't done their homework, sir.'

'Like you, Danny.'

'Like me, sir.'

'Quite. And Beaky says, "It's very simple: no do homework, no go home." And talking of going home, look at that, it's almost five o'clock. I expect you've nearly finished, haven't you, Danny?'

'I finished twenty minutes ago, sir.'

'Did you really? Well, that shows how easily you can do the work, doesn't it, when you try? Now let's have a look, Beaky, and see if Danny has got it right…You think he has? Well, mostly? Good. Beaky says you can go now. You haven't missed football practice, have you, Danny?…Oh dear!'

As the boy slips out of the room Chalky says, 'Who needs a ruler when he's got Beaky?'

Val lived in Ladbrooke Grove and so she was able to pick him up in the morning on the corner of Kensington Church Street for he was still living in the little room in the little house in the little street behind Camden Square.

Her car was an old red Mini and its heater didn't work. Johnny fed her breakfast as they headed south, the toast and coffee she had brought with her, her left hand reaching out – was it for the gears or the toast? Or a match to light the cigarette with? It was a large hand, soft but ringed with chunks of bilious stone heavy enough in appropriate circumstances to qualify as offensive weapons. Her fingernails – what colour would they be today? Coral? Green? Dried blood? And how would she be wearing her hair? Above her large brown eyes with their long eyelashes she had a high forehead and a mass of long brown hair that was rarely organised the same way two days running. ('An entire evening just to wash your hair! Why is it girls make such a thing about their hair?' Johnny'd asked Melissa one hot naked night in Delhi not six months back.) Val's hair might be swept up into a nest on top unreliably held in place with whatever instruments came to hand: hairpins, kirby grips, elastic bands, a prongy thing really designed for holding onions in place while you sliced them, and, one day, huge bright-blue knitting needles.

'Well, how do you like it?'

'Errmm…'

'Go on. "The intellectual's first responsibility is to truth". '

'Coo-er! Who says?'

'Noam Chomsky.'

'Sounds like a Chinese dish.'

'American philosopher.'

'Oh, right! Well, the truthful answer –'

'Just tell me they're great. Weird but great.'

'The truthful answer is they make you look like a geisha girl who's lost her touch. What about an alice band?'

Val nearly choked on her toast. 'And look like Christine Keeler? No thanks!'

So Johnny never knew, in addition to whether she would turn up on time or indeed at all on those bitter January mornings – for the little old car was not a good starter and Val had never heard of antifreeze until Johnny bought her some as part contribution to the cost of travel – so in addition to that he never knew what she would look like. It was as if she had a range of different editions of the same book and it was a matter of which edition of herself she chose to present. Johnny liked them all.

'Do you fancy coming to the Roundhouse tonight?' she asked.

'What for?'

'The Dialectics of Liberation Congress.'

'The what!'

'Marcuse is going to be there, Ginsberg, Stokely Carmichael. It's big, Johnny.'

'Think I'll stay home and brush up on Blake.'

'Ah! "Rise up, O Young Men of the New Age. Set your forehead against the ignorant Hirelings".'

'Crikey!'

'That's all the Blake I know.'

Luckily Johnny was ahead of her in that respect for the Norm had astonished him by saying, 'How would you like some Oxbridge work?'

There was an Oxbridge class at Outram Park Comprehensive!? The class numbered two, Tony and Sheila. Tony was soft spoken and thoughtful; how on earth had he survived educationally through six years of Outram Park? Well, of course it had been a grammar school when he started. Sheila, when she was sitting down, exposed so much virginal thigh it was hard to look anywhere else but she was focussed entirely on her work.

One chilly morning Val's Mini conked out at Notting Hill Gate. Johnny saw her, voluminous in black, walking towards him as he waited. It had begun to snow.

'No school today,' she said. 'Your place or mine?'

His.

'Ooh, posh,' said Val as he led her guiltily into the basement kitchen via the area.

'She'd chuck me out if she knew you were here. Luckily she's away. Jamaica, on the proceeds of me.'

'Is that why it's so cold? Let's have a cup of coffee.'

'I'm allowed one, for breakfast.'

'Tight arse.'

'Her or me?'

'Let's find out.'

'All right.'

She still had her coat on, a big ugly black thing. 'And

where's your room, then? The guest suite with satin bedspread, I expect.'

'It's there.' Johnny pointed with a teaspoon.

'But it's tiny. It's a converted store cupboard!'

'It's six quid a week.'

'Let's go to bed,' she said. 'And keep warm.'

They climbed in fully clothed but for their coats which they draped over the eiderdown; Johnny's old school duffel and her witches' cloak. His and hers. There was only room for the both of them if they lay on their sides. Val's front was folded into his back and he looked out of the little window at the snow falling into the yard. It was a far cry from Delhi. Snug, though. Some of her hair strayed on to his and he breathed it in. Her top arm was slung over him and he held her hand. With all those rings it was like holding a bag of warm bolts.

'Not much of you, is there?' she said, nursing her large warm round knees into the back of his thighs.

'Whereas –'

'Whereas there's quite a lot of me – I know. All the better to hug you with.' She had slipped her nether arm under his neck to come up the other side so that there was now a collection of four hands at his chest. 'I wonder what Blake's wife was like,' she mused.

'Bit of a mouse, I should think, living with that madman.'

'Madman? He was the only sane man of his century in England. It was all that formality and decorum and Latin that was mad.' Val had caught Blake off Johnny and in no time was in a fever. 'He was a man for our times. He was a lover of freedom. How can that be mad?'

Johnny said, 'He wouldn't prune his vine because he didn't like to interfere with natural growth. Consequently it yielded no fruit.'

'He was an apostle of free love.'

'But he didn't practise it.'

'He was a pacifist.'

'But when that poor soldier Schofield came begging in his red coat Blake assaulted him, nearly killed him. I'm all in favour of building the new Jerusalem, though.'

' "In England's green and pleasant land" eh? You and the WI then. I'm going to have some trouble with you, I can tell,' she said. 'You haven't got the right attitudes at all. You don't seem to mind a bit of free love, though.'

Johnny was licking her fingers and slipping her rings off one by one.

'Are you robbing me?' she asked.

'No, stripping you.'

'Fine. I work better with nothing on.'

On Saturday they went to try and find Danny.

'You know where he lives?' asked Johnny.

'Roughly. I know the area, I know some of the people. I'll ask around.'

Johnny didn't know the area, didn't know the people.

'Supply teachers never know the locality,' she said. 'No wonder they don't survive.'

Johnny had never before thought of a school as having a locality. People came to the school from it mattered not where; the school was its own locality.

Val said, 'It's like parachuting into the Amazon jungle with a suit and a briefcase.'

'Lucky I've got a good guide then,' said Johnny emolliently.

She certainly seemed to know her way around. First call the corner shop, get some fags.

'Always open, is Art's,' she said, pulling in and parking half on the pavement, half on the road. 'Watch out for the traffic warden.'

When she got out the two men releasing racing pigeons from basket cages ogled her. Not surprising, the way she looked. Johnny too followed her with his eye into the shop. I'm a lucky man, he thought, I don't care what we do or where we go.

A woman with black candyfloss hair and rearranged eyebrows came out with a paper bag to get carrots from a crate next to one occupied by a tortoiseshell cat.

'Poor old Art,' said Val, returning. 'No wonder he lives on Guinness and communism – only things to keep him going.'

'And the woman with the black hair?'

'That's Diane. Retired prostitute. Couldn't afford the bus fare to Piccadilly so joined the Salvation Army and –'

'Shut up, I'm cold. Let's get back to bed.'

'Not yet.' Val suddenly slid the window back. 'Oy, Pete!'

A little boy in shorts was skipping across the street.

'Wha'?' he shouts back.

'Mum at home?'

Pete, with a self-conscious but expert gesture takes a drag on his cigarette. 'David!' he calls. 'Mum home?'

David has a red face and blond hair. He walks down the middle of the road kicking a can. In tow he has a very small boy with a baby's bottle hanging from the corner of his mouth like a cigarette. He doesn't know either, or can't be bothered to say.

'One of our customers, is he?' Johnny enquires.

'Oh, he's special school, he is, right little delinquent.'

'Too rough for Outram Park, eh? Blimey!'

'He was terrorising the street at the age of three, adults included, so they say.'

'But not such a terror he can't be put in charge of toddlers?'

'That's his little brother. He'd die for him – or more likely kill for him.'

'Ready-made career as bodyguard then.'

It is true Johnny knows nothing of such streets, such people. The worst he's seen in his life (apart from India, of course) is the area behind the gasworks in Lensfield, his Surrey home town, where his mother used to take him on WRVS dinners but that was just unshaven old men in braces. Poor but tame. This, however, was partly poor and not very tame.

'Vicky's husband is a croupier,' says Val. 'He works nights.'

'Big family?'

'Just the one kid. They want a decent standard of living.'

'Where are the West Indians?'

'Not here.'

'Mum's at Vicky's,' a voice yells across the road, and off they go.

In amongst the terraces there are high-rise blocks. 'The expensive council flats,' Val explains.

'How can they live up there', Johnny wonders aloud, 'in those aerial prisons? All they've got is a view.'

'In addition to central heating and an indoor toilet.'

Johnny thinks, But no popping out to pick a sprig of mint in the backyard, no turning your palm up to the sky to see whether it really is raining. No trotting across the road in your pink furry slippers to get a packet of sugar at Art's. Nothing to do but watch telly and dream of winning the pools.

And then there's the Peabody buildings, where Vicky lives. They're not terraces of back-to-backs, they're not high-risers. They're blocks of flats, four or five floors, grey brick, separated by expanses of tarmac. Lots of them, block confronting block.

They park alongside other cars under a washing line that flaunts underwear in an icy wind. ' "No bicycling or roller-skating allowed," ' Johnny reads a sign off the broken-glass-topped wall they face. ' "The superintendent has the power to stop any games that he considers dangerous or a nuisance." Umm, sounds fun.'

But there's a fenced-in expanse of pinkish gravel on which some boys are playing football. Two larger boys have got the ball and are passing it to one another up and down the pitch while the more numerous younger boys swear and shout at them but do nothing to get their ball back and turn their attention to a dwindling snowman which they kick instead.

'Hello, Danny,' says Val, getting out of the car and pulling her black coat around her.

Danny is one of the bigger boys. He relinquishes his claim on the ball and wanders over. It is the same Danny as the one Chalky White had in detention with Beaky. His expression talking to Val and accepting her offer of a cigarette is the same as he had in the classroom that day, that is, he has no expression. It is not as if the light of his face has gone out, more as if there was never any light there in the first place.

'So, given up school as a bad job then, Danny?' she asks, proffering the match.

Johnny leaves them to it and wanders away. He feels as if he is in a prison yard. Through high fencing he sees a little garden dotted with tombs. One of the tombs is more like a railed vault.

Tombstones white as bones are stacked upright against the boundary walls, like cards. The inscriptions have mostly flaked away. There is a bench but of course nobody sitting on it this weather. Ideal location for the filming of *Bleak House*, he thinks. After a while she joins him.

'So do you reckon he'll come back to school then?' he asks.

'Maybe,' she says. She looks grey and cold now, dispirited.

' *Je suis, tu es, il est*,' says Johnny. 'How on earth would a child living here make anything of learning that?'

'On top of which he's dyslexic,' says Val. 'Dyslexics can't cope with English, let alone French. Why should "*es*" be pronounced "*ay*"? And why should it matter?'

They stand together but not touching. She has almost disappeared down inside her black coat as if it were bedclothes.

Johnny says, 'I feel as if I'm in a prison looking out on to another one.'

'What do you think it's like for the people living here then? That's why school is important – it's their ticket out. Trouble is, they see school itself as just another prison.'

'Hmm. This Peabody a philanthropist, I suppose?'

'Yes. Wonderful word, "philanthropist", isn't it? First you squeeze the poor and then you give them back a drop or two of the pints you've drawn off them. That way you stay rich and salve your conscience at the same time.'

'Yes. Still, better than not giving anything back, I suppose.'

'God! You can be bloody smug sometimes,' she snaps.

'Sorry.'

'*Bloody* smug! I expect you agree with the old guard at school: "Don't be good to them – life isn't going to be." How do you like that, Mr Classical Scholar from Surr-eh? How do you like that for a philosophy of education?'

'I don't. It's terrible, obviously, but –'

'Here you are, about to trot back to cosy Kensington, you've finished your slumming for the day and so let's get back to real life with my Oxford friends, hwah, hwah –'

'I'm not. I'm with you –'

'Don't you see what a totally shitty system it all is? How bloody unfair?'

'Yes, that's why –'

'*Fuck* the system, I say! Fuck so-called civilisation, fuck the arts, fuck politics, fuck business, just blow the whole fucking lot to bits and start again – if you can be bothered.'

Hair all over the place, gearstick hand a gemstone knuckle-duster. Val's anyway erratic driving is not improved by this tirade. A car hoots behind them at the traffic lights.

'*Fuck you too*,' she suddenly shouts, slamming back the sliding window and offering a generous V-sign. She swivels round to face Johnny. ' So now you know what it's like and now you know what I think and you obviously think I'm a lousy driver and a thoroughly "common" person so why don't you just get out here?'

'Val, we –'

'Take a taxi, why don't you? Driver probably lives in a Peabody building, working all hours, cheated and insulted by his passengers, paying half his earnings to the capitalist bastard who owns his cab and does fuck-all for his money.'

'Val, we were going to have supper together.'

'Well, we're not now. So get out and take your nasty upperclass capitalist shitty ideas with you. I'm waiting.'

So was the traffic behind her, not patiently as the lights were green. Johnny got out to avoid further trouble – with anyone – and the little car shot off, its cracked exhaust blowing a smoky raspberry at him as it went. Bloody hell – Sloane Square!

It was a long walk home.

But when he got there she was waiting for him.

'Boiled egg, anyone?' he said, leading her in.

After which she fell to feasting on him. Narrow though the bed was they extended its operating capabilities by pushing it away from the wall so that limbs might overhang both sides. Her wide mouth and pliable lips had the full-strength suction of an industrial vacuum cleaner but also the softness of the inside of an oyster. She played on this range with inventiveness and brio, bringing to sensual life some parts of his body he had not hitherto considered for inclusion in his catalogue of what she called 'erogenous zones'. He hadn't thought that he and Melissa had overlooked anything. He hardly liked to think of what she was doing where but goodness it worked! She for her part didn't mind if her osculations and glottalisations brought him to a sudden unilateral conclusion, for she not only knew how to play upon him but also how to get him to play upon her, in ways he had not previously thought of, and to her immense and vociferous satisfaction.

'The way to remain in control is to put everything out for the sake of one child,' she said. Oh, right – they were back to education. That was quick. She was lying on top of him now, heavy and sweating, like a leopard sprawled along a branch for ease of digestion. 'That's what Eddy would say and that's what I try to do.'

'Not so difficult when you're teaching one-to-one as you are.' He envied her that. Let her try it with a class of thirty-five. What are the other thirty-four doing?

'The old-fashioned teacher will say, "Identify the ringleader. Get the better of him, The rest will fall into line".'

'A sort of execution then. Chop off the head and you'll get little trouble from the body.'

'To them it's a fight. One victor, one victim. But I say *win* the head. It's not about showing them you're the boss, you're stronger than them because you're an adult and cleverer and can hit them if you want to. It's about being down there with them, showing you can take it, that they can throw what they like at you and you'll still be there – for them, not for yourself. That's what strength is and that's what they'll respect.'

'Hmmm. Very Christ-like,' said Johnny, unsure whether he could actually face the Calvary route. Going courageously to a voluntary death was no guarantee of resurrection. And anyway how long could you go on 'taking it'? For how long would you still 'be there'?

'One day the kids had a great riot in the playground. Somebody dropped a bottle of lemonade and it went off bang so they grabbed other bottles off other kids and chucked them high up in the air so that when they came down they made an even bigger and louder explosion, bubbles, liquid, glass everywhere. They had a great time. Now what would you do about that?'

'Well, I'd stop it if there looked like being injury. Otherwise wait, then when it was all over I'd get the whole school in and say, "Right, school caretaker can't clear that lot up, everybody out and pick up the pieces".'

'All the kids? All the pieces? And have them cutting their hands and bringing in slivers of glass for God knows what purposes for the rest of the day? What Eddy did, he let it run its course. When the last bottle had gone and the excitement died away, the bell went and the kids trooped into school for another day in the classroom. He takes assembly as usual, the kids are quiet, waiting for the backlash. But it doesn't come. There's no mention of lemonade or broken glass. It's as if the episode hadn't happened. Then when the kids have all gone off to class Eddy goes out with a broom and starts cleaning up the mess, all on his own, no staff, no caretaker.'

'Big job.'

'He's at it from nine till 10.45. At break the doors to the school buildings are locked, no one allowed out, and he carries on. They can see him working away out there. Then a bunch of kids goes to the staffroom and says, "We'd like to help Mr Eddington, please let us out."

"Not sure if he needs any help," says the teacher, "I'll ask."

Of course by this time there are kids hanging out of every window on that side of the building.

"Some of the children would like to help clear up," calls the teacher. "Shall I let them out?"

"Yes, if they'd really like to," Eddy calls up, "but there aren't any more brushes."

"They say they'll use their hands."

"Well, they'll have to be careful."

In two minutes flat half the school is in the playground and the teachers have to shut the doors on the other half or there'll be so many they'll be trampling on the glass and making it worse. Every chunk, every shard, every sliver they pick up and put in the bin. By the end of break, when they've sluiced down the whole playground with buckets – making a line, you know, from the tap at the back as if they were putting out a fire – that playground's cleaner than it's ever been in its life. All the kids not taking part are watching every move. They'd give anything to be out there. Later in the day anyone with a plaster where they got cut – they might as well be wearing a VC.'

'Well, well.'

'And that's not all. At the end of school there's Eddy just inside the school gate with a crate of lemonade bottles he's bought with his own money. "Anyone who lost a bottle this morning help themselves to a replacement." No one touches them. Next morning a huge dad barges in – "My boy's got cuts on his fingers, says he's been picking up broken glass." The man has a knife himself.

"Yes," says Eddy. "He volunteered to do it. He's old enough to decide such a thing for himself."

When the man hears the whole story he stomps out saying to a bunch of kids in passing, "You do what that man wants or I'll slice your ears off." '

The following week Johnny approaches his lesson with 3c in a more than usually despondent frame of mind. They fill him with dread, do 3c. As he walks from one school site to another he always hopes that something will suddenly happen to prevent his arriving at the other place and having to face the class; perhaps there'll be a road accident that he would have to attend to and so have an excuse for not turning up. This time he thinks, 'I could just keep on walking, walk past the school into the High Road, down to the Tube and away, cheeri-bloody-o to Outram Park, to hell with you, 3c, you can find someone else to torment, I've had enough.'

But he doesn't. Duty calls. Pride calls, and what on earth could he say to Val? What would she think of him? More importantly, would she go on being his?

It is clear, though, as he approaches the classroom there is more than the usual mayhem going on. Ma Boardman obviously hasn't been by that way to shut them up. His heart sinks further. He enters the room. It is absolute pandemonium. Then suddenly an odd thing happens. The panic and rage that was just about to blow him apart does a complete somersault and a feeling of calm courses through him. It is as if he had prepared to enter the storm with every kind of protection – hat, mac, boots, umbrella – and then thought, Oh what the hell – I'm going to get soaked anyway so why not chuck off this lot and be done with it. So he's down to his shirt and trousers and soaked to the skin in seconds but – hey – who cares about getting wet, it's easy to dry off afterwards, quite bracing really. Relax, man.

He closes the door behind him and goes to his desk, sits down. Most of the children haven't even noticed him but one or two of the quieter ones who aren't joining in glance at him quizzically. What's he on to then? Johnny is careful not to catch anyone's eye but surreptitiously he takes in the scene. They're flicking stuff about. What? There's an odd smell in the air. Putty? A beige pellet pings across his open register on the desk. Yes, it's putty and they're getting it from one of the windows. Obviously there's been a breakage and a replacement and not time enough for the putty to set so they're picking it out and flicking it around, balling it up, rolling it out between their palms and making snakes of it, stuffing it in each other's ears if they can. It's total mayhem, Abel the ringleader, as usual.

Johnny sits on. He has two worries. One is that a member of staff will come in because of the row and see him abjectly sitting there while the boys run riot ('That new supply lad's had it.') The other is that they might turn their fire on him and then he'll have to do something about it. Or will he? What would Val advise? What would Eddy do?

'Yer not gonna teach us then, sir?' a boy asks.

'I don't think the class is teachable at the moment,' Johnny replies, not looking up.

'Why don't yer stop them, sir?'

Johnny doesn't answer. 'Because I can't,' is something he cannot say, except quietly to himself. What was the first duty of an intellectual according to that Chopsticks chap of Val's? To truth. Well, that was the truth. So there. To pretend was to be at the mercy of fear. He was lost, hopeless and floundering, but he was not afraid.

Mayhem continues. Johnny is at work.

'Watcha doing, sir?'

'I'm writing a poem.'

'Cor! You a poet then?'

'No more than you are. I expect you've written poems.'

'Nah! I'm no good.'

'Nor am I,' says Johnny. 'Give me a rhyme for "putty".'

'Nutty.'

'Smutty.'

'Futty.'

'Farty.'

'Potty.'

'That's not a rhyme.'

'Is nearly.'

There are several boys at it now, even one or two of those still engaged, though now half-heartedly, with the putty.

'Sir's writing a poem about putty,' one of them announces over his shoulder to the dwindling mêlée.

'No, I'm not, I'm writing a poem about Abel.'

Abel, a large Jamaican boy, is keeping the flame of mischief well alight still.

'Hey, Abel, he's writing a poem about yer.'

'Yeah?' Abel looms up, scattering the weak, two lengths of putty depending from his broad nostrils like stalactites of snot.

' "There was a young fellow called Abel..." ' Johnny begins, eyes firmly on his work. 'Give us a rhyme for "Abel".'

'Table.'

'Label.'

'Stable.'

'Cable.'

'OK, OK. "There was a young fellow called Abel, Who..."'

' "Stuffed his mum under the table".'

' 'ere watch it!'

' "Who always wore a label".'

' "Who kept a 'orse in a stable".'

'My dad's got a 'orse.'

'Yeah, Steptoe's 'is name, innit?'

There is a group rendition of the theme tune.

'OK,' says Johnny, 'now comes the difficult bit.'

Indeed limericks prove too difficult. Clerihews then.

'All it's got to do is rhyme, never mind about the metre.'

'What's the meter got to do with it?'

'Electricity meter.'

'Gas meter.'

'Put a bob in the slot.'

'I said never mind about it. Right. "Abel James/Fell in the River Thames/when they got him out..." '

' "He had snot coming out of his snout".'

' "They said What a lout!".'

' "He ate a sprout".'

' "He gave them a clout".'

'I'm not doing poetry,' says Abel, disgruntled.

'No one says you have to.' Most of the class now are. 'What are you going to do then?'

'Nothing.'

'OK. I hope you don't get bored.'

'I ain't bored.'

'Well if you do get bored by any chance you might like to put that putty back where it came from. I don't think the window will be very safe without it.'

'I'm not a bloody window mender.'

'Nor am I but we'll need to find someone here who can do it before we leave if you can't.'

'Didn't say I can't.'

'Prove it then,' pipes a poetry-writing boy bravely.

Abel snatches the putty from his nostrils. ' 'ere, you, give us yer putty...and you...'

By the time the bell goes the putty, or most of it, has been replaced, very badly – it is all fingerprints and indentations and a lot has gone missing – but it is back where it should be. Leaving the room, Abel throws a furtive glance over his shoulder at his handiwork.

'Well, it's a step forward, isn't it?'

'Yes,' says Val. 'Now prepare for the two steps back.'

'Oh, thanks!'

'And then the two or three steps forward again. That's how it goes. Takes time.'

What confidence she gave him, so bold she was and making love to him like a tigress! 'I could eat you, Johnny Clarke,' she declares. (Does she say that to all of them?)

Johnny is no longer in the little room in the little house because his landlady has come home, smelled a rat and foreclosed sharpish on his tenancy. Hope auntie doesn't get to hear.

Angus (old school mate) says, 'You can join us lot.' He lives in a flat above the Bayswater Road, traffic passing day and night like a river in spate through a canyon. 'You'll have to share with Tosser.'

'Tosser?'

'Tony Prosser. Doing articles. Nice bloke.'

Tosser isn't in till late so Johnny and Val have the room to themselves after school.

'What did the staff make of Eddy then?' he asks. They're in bed, as usual, keeping warm.

'It was love him or hate him. Split down the middle. The trads felt betrayed. If they sent a boy to the head it was to have him beaten. They didn't want him coming back thirty minutes later with his hands in his pockets and a grin on his face having had a packet of crisps and a friendly chat with Eddy. Albie, Chalky – that lot, they'd say, "These boys are beaten at home, that's the way they're brought up. If we don't beat them they won't understand and they won't behave." Then the new lot, my sort, we say, "Yes, they get beaten at home, our job is to show them something different, something better. What's civilisation about? What's education for? No more beating, we say, let's have an end to violence".'

'Difficult for the children, though, surely. One thing at home, another at school?'

'Worse than that, they had both at school. Of course, they were quick to work out which teachers were the beaters and which were the talkers, but it was upsetting for them, always on edge, switching from one climate to another. One day when I came into school I found a boy crouched in the corner of the room. Christ – he'd been there all night! Hadn't dared go home because he'd cheeked his dad, his dad had belted him and threatened to kill him, (so he said) so at the end of school he hid himself away and got locked in. There he was, shivering and weeping in his underpants because he'd peed himself because he'd been too frightened to go out of the room into the school to the toilets. I went to Eddy, what should I do? "Right now you're his parent," he said. "What do you think you should do?" So I went out, bought a new pair of pants and a hot bacon roll. He stayed with me all day except when Eddy was talking to him. At the end of the day he went home with a letter he'd written to his dad apologising for cheeking him.'

'And if they didn't live happily ever after,' commented Johnny, 'that was at least some little bright light in the darkness, wasn't it? Like you and Danny. Maybe Danny won't come back to school. Maybe he'll never be happy. But he may always remember how one cold slushy day his teacher – what was her name now, big, sexy girl? – came all the way down from London to talk to him and give him a cigarette. But this Mr Eddington – what happened to him? Why did he go?'

'They got rid of him.'

'Who? Why?'

'The governors, backed up by a few staff who made it their business to feed things to them.'

'Lies?'

'Half-lies – things that could be conveniently twisted to look bad. For example, a boy calls one of the dinner ladies a "silly cunt". Eddie has him in. "Do you know what a cunt is, Billy?" "Well, it's...er..." No, he doesn't know. Eddie shows him a diagram in a book. So how does that come out?'

' "Headmaster shows pupils dirty pictures".'

'Quite. So they undermined him, the teachers; the governors, they under-resourced him, went behind his back, determined to get rid of him, he was too much trouble. Local press picks it up. County Hall get involved. There's a "hearing" – more like a bloody inquisition. His position becomes "untenable" – he leaves, of his own accord, for the sake of the school.'

'No wonder the school's in such a mess now. Val, what

are you doing?'

It was clear what she was doing. She was sitting up and palpating her left breast.

'I'm checking for lumps,' handling her mammary with the businesslike objectivity of a greengrocer thumbing a melon for ripeness.

'Lumps? Lumps of what?'

'Cancer of course. It's the latest thing. Breast cancer.' She made it sound like a fashion. Odd thing about her, Johnny thought, she is completely without sexual self-consciousness and yet with all the make-up and health concerns she's fussy as can be about her body as if it might dissolve beneath her unless she's doing something to maintain it.

'Anyway, it's my turn for rebirthing tomorrow,' she said.

'I've heard of resurrection,' said Johnny, 'but being born again is new to me. Or have you gone Hindu?'

'We've done it for Dee and she says it's fabulous. You're in the dark, naked, and you cover yourself with oil and curl up in the foetal position on the floor. Then the other people around you –'

'This is your "circle" you've talked about before?'

'That's right.'

Although Johnny was with Val now virtually all the time he was aware that there was in her usual social life a group of people of similar persuasion to her own, people with whom she went to congresses on the dialectics of liberation and suchlike, people not like him. Perhaps she didn't want him introduced to that circle; he was sure he didn't want to be part of it. Him and her, that's all he wanted. To hell with Marcuse and co.

'Anyway, what happens is, the other people around you, they all urge you on, they whisper encouragement and sigh and breathe in and out, "ooh…aah", and you have this incredible feeling of love and life being beamed on to you, being swirled around like amniotic fluid.'

'No touching involved then?' queried Johnny, a little uneasy at the thought of his girlfriend's oiled flesh being manhandled by strangers. Her being naked was bad enough. Did they believe in free love, these circle people? – he didn't like to ask that either.

'No touching, just voices, and you imagine yourself being born, but gently this time, not that sudden last shove and the crying and the blood that goes with ordinary human birth.' Clearly Val and her circle considered that they had invented a superior alternative to the traditional and familiar method. 'No, you just gently, slowly unfold and gradually light comes on, the people around you are lighting candles from each other around you as a symbol of new life, again nothing violent or sudden. There's music in the background, soft African music playing, music that goes straight in with your heartbeat, straight into your bloodstream, you feel it on your pulse, it's lulling you but at the same time pouring life and spirit and energy into your body and mind.'

'I expect joss sticks come into it too,' contributed Johnny not unsceptically.

'You bet. So that everything around you – sight, sound, smell, oh! and taste because as your eyes come slowly open you open your mouth too and the people around you put droplets of sweet stuff on your lips and your tongue. That way coming into the world is the most wonderful experience instead of all screams and fear.'

'Right, and what this achieves is?'

'It gets you over the trauma of your first birth, and not just the birth but, before that, the implantation of that first cell, that tiny little survivor of the holocaust of millions of sperms, swimming their frantic, competitive, survival-of-the-fittest journey to the ovary. And that trauma, you know, in that miniscule cell communicates itself to all the ensuing cells that develop from it, the cells that go to make us.'

'I'm just one big multi-cellular trauma, then?'

'We all are. The whole human race is. That's why we're all so fucked up and the world is so full of violence and injustice. Getting reborn as individuals is the start to getting reborn as peoples, as a race.'

'Wow! Anyway, Blake would have approved, I should think.'

'He certainly would. You can come along if you like.'

Val's 'circle' was certainly not his, but then did he have a circle at all and, if so, what was it? Where was he in the wild party in full swing all around him and in which Val seemed to be one of the leading dervishes? He hadn't thrown away his tweed jacket in favour of flowers and geometric shapes and he hadn't grown his hair long. He didn't take drugs – did Val and her circle take drugs? – again he didn't dare ask – and though active in pre-marital sex he was (unlike Val) not without guilt about it (though that didn't make it better) and not promiscuous (though that did) for he made love only where he loved already. Then he hadn't exchanged Christianity for atheism, existentialism or some oriental form of meditation, and he wasn't convinced that turning the world upside down would make it feel any better. In fact he thought it would make it feel thoroughly sick, all the blood would rush to its head, its money would come jingling out of its pockets and there would be murderous chaos while it tottered dizzily about in an effort to regain its balance and rediscover its sense of direction.

'You're so bourgeois, Johnny,' Val would taunt him, smiling. 'You're an upper-middle class sugar mouse and I could eat you whole.'

That he was only middle, not upper-middle class, and that she had well and truly eaten him whole already was the best riposte he could muster. Anyway that was much nicer than her earlier tirade about privilege and capitalism and 'the system'. What did she *really* think?

And what was *his* circle? Angus and his mates, drinking, womanising, doing their articles and destined for marriage and respectability in a couple of years? No revolution there, for sure. Not even looking for new answers in a new world, just a merry few rounds before last orders and being turned out on to the street of family and career and pension. For Johnny, though a rebirth was not for him, there must be more to life than that.

And so he turned to Rawle.

Having been treated by Val to a Saturday in search of Danny in South London, why didn't he treat her to a rather different weekend?

He remembered taking Jane, his first girlfriend, to Rawle

soon after she had gone up to Cambridge and was twinkling with socialist excitement. It was embarrassing. She cringed at everything about the place and its people, whether it was the Nidds themselves who had been there for nine hundred years or those who served them so feudally, its richness of land and buildings – and yet it was shabby. 'A stately home and there's no heating! He's a lord and his shirt collar's frayed!' The dining table groaned with silver and plate but the napkins, monogrammed and stiff as cardboard, had been darned. Lord Nidd pinched out the candles the moment dinner was done, complaining at the cost of them, though they burned in candelabra worth thousands. And she argued politics with her host. And she refused him, Johnny, her boyfriend of two years' standing, her bed, preferring to cosy up to the latest edition of *New Briton*. It was the beginning of the end for them.

Would something similar happen with Val?

In the event just the opposite. They arrived late one chilly Friday evening, the Mini having let them down only once en route. Then, whereas new guests were normally overwhelmed by the slaverous greeting of the Rawle pack, Val was all over them, pulling into her arms any animal that came within reach, and kissing it. To Lord Nidd she took instantly, as he to her. It was as if she'd come to a party but was the hostess at the same time and enjoying it more than anyone. And that night, instead of refusing him her bed as Jane had done, she sought him out before he'd got his slippers on to find her himself, and they weren't even on the same floor, he as usual in 'Anglesey', ('Johnny's room') up the back stairs, and she on the family floor.

'Aren't you glad to have me?' she asked, snuggling in, sensing his reserve.

He wanted to say, 'I hope no one saw you or heard you'; but she would say, 'Who cares? They don't think I'm your *sister*, do they?'

Onjon (though absent on this occasion) and his new fiancée Roberta had separate rooms, he knew, and if they sidestepped that convention it was done discreetly. 'But discretion is suppression,' as Val had once opined, 'and suppression is death.'

And then that aphorism from Blake about it being better to murder an infant in its cradle than nurse unacted desires… 'But that's one of the Proverbs of Satan,' Johnny countered. 'Bah!' was her response, acting her desire with relish.

'Only one way to get warm now,' she said, peeling off the bedsocks he had advised her to bring and putting her feet to work on him in that way peculiar to her that never failed to get him on the move. Anyone sleeping underneath must have known about it. He rather hoped it wasn't Fi.

The next day, clear and bright and cold but not freezing, Lord Nidd happily undertakes to show Val around the place. As Onjon and Fi between them take more and more contol of the estate and its burgeoning business Lord Nidd, beginning to roll on an arthritic hip, plays increasingly the part of benign patron, taking time to chat to people, pouring oil on waters troubled by his children's drive for change and development. If the home farm is to go in for rare breeds, Reg, the cowman, is going to have to have time away to procure them. A couple of days down in Herefordshire leaves the herd in need of attention so Lord Nidd will fill in for him, 'make myself useful'. It is also he who has put time into researching apples, discovering (to everyone's delight) in their own horticultural archives the existence of a fruit called the Rawle Red, no longer growing on the estate but hanging on to life and taxonomic recognition in the apple research place in Kent. There it has been carefully grafted and is now filling the gaps in the orchard that had like so much else fallen into neglect, brambles and white willow happily growing up into the branches of the old trees whose fruit, few and grub-infested, fell to the ground to be pecked by blackbirds, to go brown and bungy in autumn, black and soggy in winter.

Fi with her father's and Milton's help has saved the orchard. In among the older trees, some of which have been grubbed up and others hard-pruned, she has planted robust little specimens of the home fruit, the Rawle Red, its root firm in bonemeal and compost, its supporting stake twice its own frail thickness, its tender stem protected from rabbits by plastic tubing. And now, the sap well sunk, it's time for the annual prune. Johnny is helping Fi.

She has been quiet so far this weekend. Well, she's always quiet but, as Johnny has noticed before, the more guests there are the less conspicuous she is – unless conspicuous by her silence or her absence. She is not blatantly antisocial but always has something to attend to: the chickens must be shut up for the night, she needs to take one of the dogs to the vet – and she prefers to go alone. It's not that she has no small talk – she has virtually no talk at all. On this occasion she has so far addressed not a word to Val and hardly a word to him. What does she think about all the time? Is it just Rawle and nothing else? She had steeled herself to ask him about his boys but that was the previous term.

Now she has equipped him with secateurs and told him what to do, how to distinguish between the leaders and the laterals, to be careful when pruning the tip-bearers. Johnny is happy to be her pupil and it isn't difficult. The work becomes more or less mechanical. In the absence of conversation Johnny sings, 'Oh what a beautiful morning!' Well, it is. The sky is clear, light blue. 'There's a bright golden haze on the meadow.' Well, no, not really. In fact the sun is silver and the cold grass is as crisp as a girl's beehive hairdo. Fi's hair is thick, dark, parted naturally in the middle, falling short of her shoulders; it owes nothing to the hairdresser, any more than her skin owes anything to Max Factor. She isn't singing but she might be listening.

They are making their way down the row together, sharing and alternating the tasks. Johnny might notice a branch she can't quite reach and brings it down for her, picking up her prunings and chucking them into the trailer of the little red garden tractor she drives. When she is doing that he holds her secateurs for her, their metal handles smooth and warm from her industrious grip. He wants to keep them warm for her, for when she gets back to him. The little figure driving away from him, bumping along on the tractor seat, red bobble hat bobbing up and down – as he watches her, it is as if she is re-entering an habitual solitude that he wishes to save her from but he makes no move to go with her, to keep her company. The tractor fades away. The silence seems final. He waits. She might not come back. But then the motor is heard again – she is on her way. Johnny returns to work in case she should see him just standing there, looking out for her.

When she gets back she says, 'What are you going to do?' – as if she has been brewing the question while apart from him.

Johnny feels challenged. 'About what?' But he knows what. 'Well, I expect I'll get a proper job teaching.'

'And make that your career?'

'Yes, I suppose so.' 'Career' wasn't really a concept he'd entertained before.

'You don't sound very convinced.'

'I guess I'm not a very convinced sort of person. I tend to go along with things.'

'You're very easily influenced, aren't you?'

'Yes, I am.' Johnny wishes the admission to sound assertive but it just sounds weak. 'Unlike you.'

'Me?'

'Yes. You seem to be a very convinced sort of person. Your commitment to Rawle, for example, it's very single-minded.'

'Did you say "simple-minded?" ' she queries but there is a smile in her voice. She's up a stepladder, snipping away, so he can't see her face. He's holding the ladder for safety – not that she's asked him to: for all that she's skilled and determined she needs security, he considers.

Later Lady Nidd passes by on her way to visit the London couple who pay a huge rent for the Dolls' House. 'You're doing well, you two,' she says in uncharacteristically chatty tones. Does she for some reason have 'a beautiful feeling' too? Johnny did at the outset but this unusual outspokenness of Fi's has shaken him. And yet it has somehow made him happy too. He feels confused.

The bell in the stableyard rings for elevenses and they are relieved.

On the way back to London Val can hardly contain her excitement. She has had a whale of a weekend, talking to everyone, making friends with most of them and enchanting Lord Nidd. 'He's gorgeous!' she enthuses. Lord Nidd for his part seems to have shed ten years in her company. 'And he completely agrees with me about the school.' This is what she's excited about. 'I mean what does it take to start a school?' she asks, as if it were a rhetorical question to which the answer is, 'Oh, nothing at all.' 'There's you and me, me with the special expertise and you with all the other subjects.'

'Except maths and –'

'All right, except maths. There's bound to be someone on the estate who can do sums.'

'Not a trained teacher.'

'No, maybe not but that's the whole point of the community school, isn't it?'

This is what she's calling it, because the school is a genuine part of the community in which all the adults are teachers. 'Think of Mrs Brydon cooking away. Great, excellent product, sells well, but who's learning from her? While she's working she can be teaching as she goes along. 'Right, recipe for six, requires two ounces of sultanas so if we're cooking for twenty what weight of sultanas do we need?' There's your maths. Then, sultanas, raisins, currants – what's the difference, where do they come from, how do they get like that? Geography, Biology – it's all there. That way the whole of living is learning. And Rawle has a whole new product – education!'

From this follows what can be learned from Milton and his woodcraft, Veal and his boy, the gardeners, Reg and Mick down at the home farm. The children, who are drawn from the locality, get attached in turn to the different activities going on around the place and so learn different skills. In time they specialise and, in effect, become apprenticed to a particular craft.

'We've got fixated on *schools*, those old-fashioned, institutionalised quasi-monasteries with their obsession with the abstract, the academic, or simply "results". They talk about "subjects", as if life should be broken down into theoretical sectors. But that's to put life, with all its interest and colour and variety, on to a dissecting table and examine it and do experiments on it and write reports on it. That's to treat life like a dead thing, a corpse, as if education is an autopsy. It's not right, leave alone the fact that not everyone's academic. In fact only about five per cent of the population can flourish in a purely academic environment. No wonder they kick up.'

'Your dyslexics, for example.'

'Especially my dyslexics. Exactly. Now there's a thought! We've been talking about a local school but why not bring city kids up here?'

'Like your Danny.'

'Like Danny, yes. Get him out of the prison of the classroom, broaden his horizons. Give him something to *do*.'

'And give him a taste of the country.'

'And if he doesn't take to rearing pheasants or planting trees at least he'll go back to London with some awareness of these things.'

'Even more true for those West Indian kids who've never even been into the countryside at all let alone seen what milk comes out of.'

'Absolutely!'

'But then come to think of it, not just your deprived kids. Some of the lads at Eaton House would probably take to it, or at any rate benefit from it. It would sweeten their exam work.'

'That's it, they could live here for a while. Not full-time like you and your boarding school but just for a week, say, with their teachers to keep an eye on them.'

'And the teachers would learn something too. When they go back to their town schools they've got something to work on, to follow up.'

'Right, so we're not some little privileged backwater for thickoes who are only fit for milking cows or cooking. We're a …a *centre*, yes, that's the word, a centre, like the hub of a wheel radiating out into society – that's more like it.'

And so, the A40 passing beneath the Mini's wheels, the dream is spun. Johnny doesn't like to ask, 'What about class and privilege and capitalism and all that stuff you wanted a revolution for?' The rebel Val seems to have given way to the life-loving Val: instead of chucking bricks at the upper class she's joining in the dance with gusto! Is her revolutionary fervour just envy, like your Councillor Jack Grumpy who becomes a Labour MP then to retire as Lord Grumpy of Smokeville and sit in ermine among the other 'noble lords'?

'And Lord Nidd's all for it, you say?' he now asks.

'Dead keen. Even showed me a building – used to be a battery hen shed apparently, quite spacious. That could be the school. No, not "school", we're not using that dreadful word. I mean the "centre". Of course it doesn't need to be much. The kids will be out and about most of the time doing things. We don't need rows of classrooms – thank God, I hate classrooms – the centre would be, well, one room really, yes, an open-plan arrangement, people flowing freely, mixing, sharing. Oh, and an office for you.'

'I'm the office boy, am I?'

'No, idiot! You're the organiser, the administrator. You work out who's doing what and when and all that sort of thing. Someone's got to be practical.'

'So I'm the bursar and you're the headmistress?'

'Don't be silly. We don't use words like that. "Manager" maybe.'

' "Centre Manager". Hmmm. OK so what are you doing, apart from whizzing around being enthusiastic?'

'Don't sneer, we'll need enthusiasm. This is pioneering stuff. The forces of reaction will try to pull us back. We'll have to fight them with energy and commitment.'

'OK, I'll be the boring bloke in the background. In that case I ask, what about money? What about being paid? I mean what do we – you and I – live on?'

'We live on the estate. It's all here, food and shelter. What do you need money for? Money is alienated whatever-it-is, according to Marx.'

'Clothes, fags, petrol?'

'Oh, I'll dump the car, won't need that. OK, well, I guess we'll have to charge fees a bit. Yes, those groups coming from city schools the Local Authority will have to pay for.'

'We could get businesses and charities to support us maybe,' suggested Johnny. 'Lord Nidd knows a lot of people, important, well-connected people.'

'Rich people! That's right – contacts. He'd be our patron and we'd have an appeal –'

' – set up a foundation.'

'Fantastic!'

Oh so much planning to do! So many fizzing ideas!

'Of course I'll have to get Onjon onside. Did you speak to Fi about it?'

'No.'

'Well, it's great to have Lord Nidd rooting for us but we'll need to convince both Fi and Onjon – they're the real deciders.'

'They'll love it surely. It's a natural extension of the whole Rawle concept – co-operation, community, creativity…'

While Val expected to carry all before her with enthusiasm and the force of her personality Johnny hoped to carry it with thinking and planning. 'We need a prospectus,' he said. Success could not be taken for granted. For his role in bringing the dowager to her senses so that she left her money to the family rather than to the Pilgrims he was regarded as Rawle's saviour, the family's debt to him huge and lifelong. All the more reason he should not put Onjon and Fi in an awkward position. Supposing they didn't fully believe in the educational project that he and Val were now working on day by day and believing in all the more day by day? It would be hard, with their debt of gratitude to him, to say No. Then, since his training in America, Onjon had become so professional and businesslike in his approach to the Rawle vision that he would not agree to something unless he was well and truly convinced that this educational project would fit – and enhance – that vision.

So it needed working on.

'Agriculture…'

'…dairy, arable, poultry.'

'Horticulture…'

'…veg, fruit, flowers.'

'Arboriculture…'

'…commercial exploitation of woodland.'

'Pisciculture…'

'Eh?'

'Fishes.'

'Oh.'

'Commercial trout farm maybe, or management of recreational angling amenity. These things are all there, or in the blueprint, and they all have educational potential.'

'Oh! And equiculture.'

'That's right, don't let's forget the horses. That's Lady Nidd's department.'

'Onjon thinks that riding is going to become the great rural growth area. All those keen little girls in jodhpurs want teaching. And apparently his Roberta is a keen horsewoman too.'

'A riding school then.'

'It's in the plan.'

What they had to do was create something that was a natural extension of what was happening at Rawle already, not something at odds with the fundamental blueprint.

'What we think is,' Johnny wrote to Onjon, 'that the educational function is a natural by-product almost of what is happening anyway.' He explained the apprenticeship idea, pointing out the mutual advantage of such a scheme. 'Here, then, is the "prospectus" that Val and I have put together. Of course it's just a first shot and it's all for discussion and adaptation but it gives a pretty good idea of what we have in mind. I hope you like it. I know you haven't met Val yet and she is of course crucial to the success of the project but I can assure you she has terrific energy and commitment and enthusiasm, as I think your father can tell you. For me it goes without saying that nothing would make me happier than to be truly an active part of the great Rawle venture that you and Fi and everyone are already making into a serious success as well as something unique in England. I look forward to discussing this with you when you've got the time – and introducing Val to you, of course – so that together we can convince you, I hope, that what we propose is not only in harmony with your own plans but will add another strong and distinctive ingredient to the great Rawle recipe.'

Meanwhile things at Outram Park weren't getting any easier. A problem for Johnny was that he didn't really understand the school and this was not just because he had no experience of the state sector but because the school seemed to contradict itself. On the one hand there were boys and girls who could barely read or write and yet on the other there were Oxbridge candidates. There were some children, ill-dressed and unfed, shivering outside the school gates before they opened in the morning because they'd been kicked out of home an hour earlier, but there were also children who were brought to school by car, carrying their briefcases full of (completed) homework and an ample lunch-box. The latter they ate daintily in the designated classroom while others ate the free school lunches they qualified for on grounds of poverty or wandered round the playground eating chips from a hollowed-out half loaf of white bread.

Then there was flagrant indiscipline both inside the classroom and out and yet there was a public school type of prefect system; senior boys and girls in blazers had 'prefect' badges on their lapels and checked pupils into school in the morning. The staff were divided too so it was up to the individual teacher how she or he would teach. As Val had explained, there was the whole gamut of disciplinary style from 'Beat 'em yourself' to 'Send them to the head', to the new sort peaceably confronting offenders with the nature of their offences and so by mercy, talk and sympathy procuring amendment of life and heading off recidivism. But that took time, took knowledge and understanding of the children, their background and limitations, their language in the widest sense; it took courage and hard work. This approach was not something that a one-term tyro supply teacher could risk. As Val had warned him: one step forward, two steps back.

The problem was Pilch. Pilcher his real name but known as Pilch. Racial origin? English, plus something else hard to identify. Indian perhaps. Age? Fifteen or sixteen. Appearance? Short, thin, almost crew-cut dark hair, the beginnings of a moustache, the scars of some disease. Smallpox? (Did it still exist?) Anyway his dusky face was lightly pitted with little craters. Educational ambition and attainment? Almost nil. Never carried books or writing implements. If such were needed in class he 'borrowed' from a neighbour, skilled as he was over years of practice at evading both work and the consequences of so doing.

This Pilch had somehow become Johnny's *bête noire*, someone he could neither ignore nor deal with. He was there as Johnny turned off the light to sleep, there awaiting him in the morning. The menace. It was not that he was flagrantly ill-behaved, like Abel, nor always getting it wrong, like Danny; he wasn't violent or rude and he was not, as some boys were, bent on conflict, 'Borstal or Bust' written all over their troubled brows. It was more difficult than that. For one thing he never looked you in the eye, his rebellion a sort of hangdog sulk. For another his classmates were wary of him as if he had some potential power over them that might be to their harm. And so he was 'Pilch' and they lent him whatever he needed and kept clear of him.

Often he didn't turn up to class at all and then Johnny was relieved, because he felt he was making some headway with that group and Pilch's absence softened the atmosphere: surprising how much difference one person could make. But though relieved he also felt uncomfortable for it was his duty to report absence officially as well as follow it up personally so he couldn't just overlook it. Besides, who did this bloody Pilcher think he was to come and go as he pleased? Johnny could imagine him saying to someone, 'English? Nah! don't bother with that', and sneering at 'Clarke.' When he did turn up he was always late and usually appeared just at the moment when Johnny had got the class settled and the lesson was properly under way. Then Johnny was blowed if he was going to let this lateness simply pass but equally blowed if he was going to risk the lesson misfiring by clashing with Pilch. Of this dilemma was born frustration and of that frustration, anger.

And it was all made worse by the success Johnny was beginning to have with this particular group, which was an O level class. It was relatively small for that reason and though far from bright was characterised by good nature and a willingness to engage with the work which at present was a set book of modern poetry, much of the content of which – war, luckless rabbits in urban hutches, traffic – the pupils could supposedly relate to. Not only that but Johnny was successfully engineering a new teaching format of which he was rather proud. This involved putting the desks and chairs into a semicircle. His reasoning was this: a vital element in the work was discussion. How could you have a proper discussion if it was twenty-five against one – him over here and them over there?

Such a discussion might indeed involve just about everyone but it was only two-directional – teacher-to-class, class-to-teacher. If you were in the back row a comment by someone in the front row was probably inaudible to you so what incentive had you to listen to the teacher's response to it? The teacher was the only person effectively placed, the rest were peripheral.

So Johnny's alternative model was a horseshoe arrangement in which everyone could hear and see everyone else. No one was in front or behind and anyone could speak. Johnny was in the chair, in control (ha ha) but the motto was 'Talk to all: listen to all'. Though Bev and Tina, for example, would probably have preferred their previous role as front-row note-takers, looking up at Johnny from under heavy unnatural eyelashes and with blank expressions; and while Christos and Andy would rather have retained their identity as back-row slackers the class as a whole liked the new arrangement. For a start it was different and thus welcome. And then it involved moving the furniture which they enjoyed, or the boys did, because it was a rough and noisy business and took up time that would otherwise be given to work.

In the early stages of this experimental layout Johnny was on tenterhooks over its success or failure. It would seem to a traditionalist to be asking for trouble but at the same time it could be a winner and he was determined that it would be. So Pilch's lateness to class was particularly irritating not only because it was an interruption to the proceedings which he had painstakingly got under way but also in the manner of his entrance which, far from being a quiet and panting 'Sorry-I'm-late-sir' while swiftly taking the nearest vacant seat, was leisurely and unapologetic in word or manner. Unencumbered by any of the accoutrements of study such as books he entered slowly, almost wanderingly, like a visitor to a museum moving from one exhibit to another. He then stood and surveyed the scene reflectively like a fastidious cat calculating seating advantage. If there was no seat for him he would saunter to the back of the class, pick up a chair by its top rail and swing it into place right behind someone else.

'Into the horseshoe, please, Pilch – make room for him.' (Keep the tone light, don't let anyone see you're furious.) 'Never mind about bringing up a desk, as long as he's in the loop. He hasn't brought anything to put on the desk anyway.' (Couldn't resist that.)

Which creates another problem. In so far as it is possible to do so Pilch lounges, legs outstretched, flaunting shamelessly non-regulation shoes, one arm insouciantly thrown over the back of the chair. This cannot be as comfortable as he wishes to convey but the message is clear: This is boring and pointless, I don't know why I'm bothering with this, the teacher is a twat. Johnny ignores the message as best he can, channelling his suppressed annoyance into a fierce dedication to the task in hand, succeeding with the majority but failing with the one dissenter. He can't let it pass.

'Right, everyone had their say on *Pylons*?' He looks round. He knows pretty well who hasn't and picks them off, squeezing some sort of response even from those who would sooner have teeth drawn than speak voluntarily. He must have some sort of response, however reluctant, however inchoate. Johnny feels a monster slowly rising within him. Then, 'Pilch, I don't think you've spoken. What's your opinion?'

Pilch draws up one leg to scratch his knee. He has spent most of the lesson contemplating the soles of his unlawful footwear. The bell is about to go. Johnny, at bursting point, patiently repeats the question. 'Your opinion of *Pylons*, Pilch?'

'Eh? Wasser pylon?'

The class titters. Pilch sniggers. The bell goes. Johnny's rage retreats to its lair to fatten itself on frustration.

This can't go on. And doesn't. Johnny has a plan. As Pilch saunters in late to the next lesson Johnny looks up as if in surprise. 'Oh! Pilch, I wasn't sure you were coming today, so we've started. I'm afraid you're too late.' His tone is light and cool.

Pilch affects not to hear and proceeds as usual to pull up a chair. He can't even be bothered to pick it up and the scraping noise of its legs across the floor hardens Johnny's resolve.

'No, Pilch, as I said, you're too late. If you're going to come to the lesson you have to come on time. So you'd better be off.'

This injunction hangs in the air. Pilch doesn't like it. 'I'm 'ere now,' he mutters, settling in his chair.

'But you haven't got the book. It's no good without the book.'

'I'll borrer,' says Pilch. He's not happy at being put under pressure but he doesn't want trouble, it's too much bother.

'Right,' says Johnny, 'to get the best out of the lesson you need to be on time and you need to have your book. OK?' He is pleased with himself at avoiding the imperative of 'Don't be late or else.' Val's advice, that: avoid confrontation, don't command and don't threaten.

Pilch mutters some sort of sullen acquiescence. He makes, however, no contribution to the proceedings and Johnny doesn't press him. The class is not sure who's winning this contest. Sir has not really stood his original ground – in their opinion he should have sent Pilch away at the start. And yet he has laid down some laws that Pilch will have to abide by if Sir's line is to hold. The next lesson should be interesting.

But it isn't, because Pilch doesn't turn up at all. Johnny is secretly hoping that he has abandoned the subject altogether – maybe even left the school – but the boy's Year Master explains that difficult though he is he has a ferocious father who is determined that his son shall make a success of the schooling he himself never received in Malaya. 'He'll kill the boy if gets expelled.'

'I'll kill him if he doesn't,' thinks Johnny. To his horror and shame he recognises a great black cistern of violence in himself.

Will its vile waters rise and burst?

They do. But not as expected, not in the classroom. Johnny is on duty indoors one lunchtime. Monitoring the tuck shop queue is part of that duty. The tuck shop is mostly patronised by the younger children but older ones swagger along too. Queuing behind their juniors is infra dig so they generally queue-barge. This practice is naturally resented by those barged but it is preferable to the extortion or threats of violence to which they will be subject should they remonstrate. It is, however, 'not allowed' and the teacher on duty is expected to 'watch out for it' and 'stamp on it firmly' if it occurs.

On Johnny's duty this day it does and the perpetrator is Pilch, along with two other contemporaries whom Johnny doesn't know. 'Right, Pilcher, out of there, no barging in.' Pilch ignores him, pretends to be talking to his mates. 'I said "Out!"' No use pretending this time, Johnny's voice is loud and quivering with sudden rage. Everyone turns to look at him except Pilch who does not look up but says something quietly. Johnny doesn't hear what but Pilch's two mates do and they guffaw and other children in the queue who have also heard giggle and stare at Johnny. This is good: what's going to happen now? As if by some odd process of sonic delay Johnny now catches what Pilch said. It was 'Fuck off.' Johnny sees red, reaches over the small heads to grab Pilch by the scruff and drag him away. Should he be doing this? Will there be repercussions? He doesn't give a damn. The rage in his hands and his heart will have its turn, come what may. He yanks him across the corridor and into the nearest classroom, slamming the door behind him. Now…

Pilch, far from resisting, is cowering, hunched as if expecting blows and there is fear in his shifty eyes. Johnny lets go. He is disgusted. Mainly with himself – his hand is tainted with its own violence, the monster that he has permitted to grow within him, fear and hurt pride spreading through his soul to result in this – a pitiful and pitiable boy shielding his head from expected blows, at *his* hand. But he is victorious too. The thorn in his flesh he has wrenched out. The enemy is defeated. He feels triumphant, strong, merciful, generous, charitable – and creative.

'Pilch,' he says, 'tomorrow lunchtime you're coming down the tank with me.'

'Eh? Wasser tank?'

'The rowing tank. You're going rowing.'

'Goin' rowin'?' Pilch is at an utter loss.

Onjon enjoys this story and is surprised, as Johnny was, that rowing is on offer at Outram Park. Johnny knew there was a coach that took some children – those few who could rustle up some games kit, he imagined – off to a suburban playing field but it was only when he was pounced on in the staff room by a blond and breezy young man in a tracksuit who had somehow heard he had rowed at Oxford that he gathered the school had a rowing tradition, a hangover from its days as a grammar school perhaps, which included regular bookings of the Mortlake rowing tank and a coxless clinker four belonging to its rowing club.

'So you've lashed this wretched Pilcher to the thwarts.'

'He's a galley slave.'

'I'd like to see it.'

'His dad's thrilled, says it'll make a man of him.'

'Talking of making men…'

Ever since Johnny's arrival – Val had not been invited this time – the question of their vision for an educational strand to Operation Rawle had been hovering in the shadows and it wasn't until now, a chilly Saturday evening in the renovated billiard room, that Onjon brought the matter out into the open.

Johnny remembered, as the balls rolled in opulent silence over the immaculate baize sward of the great table, a rather different occasion during his second year at Oxford when a very drunk Onjon had explained to him, the ball veering in and out of great rents in the faded cloth, how the family was broke, how Rawle would have to go, this disaster being largely due to the dowager's decision to leave everything to the Pilgrim movement. The great room, then freezing, had now been fitted with an underfloor heating system that extended to the orangery next door where Veal's boy was developing a profitable line in orchids.

The place had in fact been turned into a snooker club open to all and run by volunteer members from the estate and the village. The former flower room on the other side from the orangery had been converted into a sort of bar, originally by the bringing in of crates of bottled beer but recently by the installation of a range of barrels cradled on brick piers under the old counters and draining boards.

The family now had an hour before the club opened.

'Snooker, by popular demand,' explained Onjon, rattling the gleaming reds into their triangular wooden nest. 'Pop says it's not a gentleman's game and I say this isn't a gentleman's club. You to break.'

'Yes. So, talking of making men,' Johnny prompts him, 'what do you think of our idea, Val's and my idea?'

'I think it's brilliant, inspired. Great prospectus by the way, thanks.'

'Fi equally impressed?' queries Johnny.

'Fi's not very happy at the moment.'

Well, Johnny knew about that for only the day before, as he learned on arrival, she had had to have Piggy put down.

'She gets upset about things like that. Well, you know Fi, a bit moody, emotional, even if she keeps it to herself. Anyway, the problem was Moot.'

'They didn't like it?' Johnny had forgotten about Moot, telling Val it was all a matter of Onjon and Fi now that they'd got Lord Nidd on their side.

'Not everybody, you know, feels at ease with other people's children. And not everybody feels they would be any good as a teacher. "Oh, I wouldn't have the patience," someone said.'

'They would if they were encouraged and supported, particularly by Val, she'd put heart into anyone. I can't tell you how she's helped me with the kids at Outram Park.'

Onjon was sighting for a tricky shot that put him at risk of an in-off and didn't immediately answer. Then, that safely achieved, he had to take the spider for a pot shot of the pink. What a sensible and sober man he had become in a few years,

Johnny thought, so different from the swearing drunkard of that earlier game, whacking the balls around the table in alcoholic abandon. Now, straightening up in the middle of his successful break, he said, 'Johnny, everyone here likes you and thinks highly of you – you're one of us – so what I want to suggest is that you have a go at Moot, you put it to them, try and persuade them. They might take it from you, if it comes over as your idea and if you're the one to set it all up and make it work.'

Only then did Johnny see the real problem. 'But the whole thing is Val's idea originally, she's the inspiration behind it, she'd make it a success, I know she would.'

'The thing is, though –' Onjon intently chalking his cue – 'not everyone thinks Val is all that well suited to Rawle.'

'Oh. So it's personal?'

'It seems to be.'

'I don't understand,' said Johnny, 'she got on so well with everyone – she got on a like a house on fire with your father! And she loved it here, she'd be a huge asset, Onjon, honestly. Of course you haven't met her, you don't know what an incredibly lively and creative person she is.'

'I realise that, but maybe not having met her makes it easier for me to make a judgement on this. It's nothing personal as far as I'm concerned. But, as I say, that's the Moot feeling so I – Fi and I – feel we should stand by that. Do think of having a go at it yourself though, if you're really convinced about the idea. We'd love to have you here, Johnny, you're a part of the place.'

'I couldn't do it by myself, Onjon.'

'Then get someone else in on it. It doesn't have to be Val, does it?'

Well, yes it did have to be Val, for the reasons he had given to Onjon. It was no use going to Moot as Onjon had suggested, no use approaching Fi about it. He knew the plan was dead. And now he had to tell her, and tell her not the truth, which was that she was rejected, but that the plan was. The truth would be impossible to her. No one scorned Val, no one failed to love or like her. Lord Nidd had practically fallen in love with her! She was so positive, so full of ideas. Her revolutionary outbursts were just fashionable bluster.

'Oh I get it,' she said. 'I see what it is.'

They were driving home from school on the last day of term through rush hour darkness. Someone had once told Johnny that women, unlike men, were quite capable of doing more than one thing at a time. This was manifestly not true in Val's case for she could not talk and drive, being both a bad driver and an impassioned talker. She had put on dark glasses, claiming that car headlights hurt her eyes 'after a few drinks' which is what the staff room had had by way of celebration of the Easter holidays. Now with great ill-luck another misfortune surfaced.

As they were driving along they both became aware of a rattly sort of noise coming from the rear of the car. There was nothing unusual about the old red Mini's making odd noises or malfunctioning in some way. What could you expect of a six-year-old vehicle with a mileometer firmly reading seventeen miles and a pair of windscreen wipers that plied erratically from side to side like a couple of arthritic tennis players? There were constant problems, made worse by Val's complete lack of the concept of car care. To her 'maintenance' meant putting in petrol when it was getting low. No other aspects of the machine were ever attended to except recently, since Johnny had been on the scene.

But this present noise was very loud and not to be ignored. Johnny said, 'Maybe I should take a look.'

'Oh, all right,' and Val pulled up on the spot regardless of traffic. Johnny leapt out, gesticulating apologetically to the inconvenienced driver behind, to inspect the back. Yes, there was a problem. The rear number plate had lost one of its fixing screws and one end of it was trailing in the road.

Johnny reported to Val. 'I can't fix it back just like that,' he said. 'We'll have to stop somewhere and do it properly.'

'We are stopped somewhere,' replied Val irritably and swinging wide the driver's door into the passing traffic she got out, wrenched the number plate completely off and got back in, tossing BCG 481 over her shoulder into the rubbish tip of the back seat.

'Val, you can't drive along without a rear number plate. The police'll stop you. It's in the Highway Code that –'

'Sod the Highway Code! That's what they failed me on last time. What does it matter what the bloody Highway Code says, as long as you can drive?'

'Val, what do you mean, "failed you on last time"?'

'The first time I nearly ran over an old lady while doing my three-point turn. They failed me on that when it was the old lady's fault.'

'Val, are you saying you haven't actually passed your test yet?'

'I've been driving for three years. I've got experience. I can drive all right, can't I?'

Johnny suppressed the answer 'No'. 'But you haven't got L-plates up. If the police stop you you'll be in real trouble, they'll demand to see your licence and when they see it –'

'Well, that'll just be bad luck on them because I haven't got a licence.'

'*What*?! But that must mean you're not insured either! Road tax – is that disc in date?' He couldn't see from inside. 'God! No, it can't be if you're not insured and licensed. Christ, Val, do you realise how serious this is! No driving licence, no road tax, no insurance! You could practically go to prison for that lot – huge fine at least. We really ought to stop, Val, it's mad to go any further. *And* you've been drinking – they won't like that either, not to mention the way you've been driving since they've been on your tail. Now park the car anywhere off the main road here, we'll take the Tube home and you can start getting the paperwork sorted out in the morning.'

And it was at that point that Val uttered those words, 'Oh I get it. I see what it is.'

'What? What is?'

'You and your posh friends. That's why they won't have me, isn't it? Not posh enough.'

'Don't be silly, that's nothing to do with it. Are they all what you call "posh" at Rawle – Milton, Mrs Brydon, all of them, are they "posh"? Are they going to be bothered because you've got a Yorkshire accent?'

'Well now doesn't that tell it all! He's such a bloody southern snob he can't even tell the difference between a Yorkshire and a Lancashire accent! We're all just "Ee-bah-gummmers" from "oop North" to you. And as for your Miltons and Brydons, they're little better than serfs.'

'They aren't. You haven't seen how Moot works.'

'Moot! What hypocrisy! It's just a fancy modern screen for the old feudal system. Just typical of you upper classes, thick as hell but crafty when it comes to preserving your own privileges. Give the proles the impression that they count, that what they say and who they are matters, then Lord and Lady Snootipoots can just carry on as before. Who does the place belong to? All of them? The hell it does! It belongs to the family – and I don't mean that in the sentimental way they use the word at Rawle to mean everyone working there – I mean the Nidds, the people whose name is on the title deeds – that is, if William the Conqueror got around to drawing any up.'

'Val, I can't believe you're talking like this. You seemed to enjoy yourself there, you got on with everyone, you had Lord Nidd at your feet, you didn't seem to mind all the –'

'And now they don't want me. Funny, isn't it? All right to have this northern lass for a week-end but have her there and seriously involved? – oh no, let's keep this in "the family".'

'I tell you it's the plan they don't go along with,' Johnny replied weakly. 'It's not about you.' But it was, it was. And Val had judged aright: Rawle didn't want her.

'Well, you're not going to see it, are you? You're so sucked up into their cosy little society which is no more than commercialism and feudalism dressed up as a modern commonwealth when really it's old imperialism. It's so hypocritical, it's so *disgusting*! D.H.Lawrence was right – you and your sort are just foul old fungi that need treading on and crushing out. Hundreds of years of having it all and now that there's a chance of losing it you get chummy with the working classes to keep them sweet. But they won't have me – me, the granddaughter of a postman in Burnley, with my "Yorks" accent – I don't fit. All right maybe if I knew my place, if I were "below stairs", but as an equal? – no fear! "Jumped up thing, thinks she's *educated* but, my *deah*, Sussex University – isn't that one of the *new* places, wah,wah! Oxford and Cambridge, they're the only *real* universities. She hasn't been to public school, you know, only grammar school and nowadays she'd probably be in one of those ghastly *comprehensives* – well, I *ask* you!" And you, Johnny, you know what, you haven't got a clue what you're doing here, have you? You were probably more at home in India – the Raj and all that, dontcha know, eh what? – than you are in bloody Balham. Here you're a creature from outer space and you have absolutely nothing to offer these kids because you've no idea what it's like to live like them and to have that sort of background and disadvantage and hardships. You are useless here and, you know what, you'll just end up teaching in one of your precious so-called public schools dedicated to keeping the rich in charge because you haven't got what it takes to teach where it really matters, where the country needs teaching talent if we're going to get anywhere at-bloody-all with making the social revolution we so desperately need. I don't know why I bother with you, you're just a waste of time, a waste of space, and as for your precious aristo friends in "Oxfordshah", well, you deserve each other, and if you think I –'

'Val, there's a police siren going behind us.'

'So what? We've all got things to do. Bloody pigs! They can overtake if they're in such a hurry.'

'Maybe they don't want to overtake. Maybe they're trying to talk to *you*.'

At which point the police car, its blue lights alternating right behind them, began to flash its headlights as well.

'Val, I really think you should pull over. They're getting impatient. It won't help your case if they think you're being unco-operative.'

'"Unco-operative!"' snorted Val, and with a sudden wrenching of the wheel she took a sharp left turn into a little side street, narrowly missing a white van attempting to get out on to the main road. 'Now he can overtake,' said Val. 'Is that "co-operative" enough for you? What a horrid word "co-operative" – just the sort of word you and your friends would use. "Oh! Let's co-operate. Let's work together. Oh, aren't we ever-so-friendly, ever-so-modern, ever-so-democratic!" *Hunh!*'

Val's rear-view mirror was permanently angled for make-up purposes, her wing mirror she'd never had a use for, but even so she could not fail to notice that the police car had not taken the opportunity she had given it to pass her on the main road, but had turned off as she had and was still right behind her, all alarm signals going.

'Val, if you don't stop I'm going to open my door and jump out!'

'Don't be stupid, you'll hurt yourself.'

'Yes, but maybe I won't die which is what is going to happen to both of us at this rate.'

Val's response was to speed up. 'Their problem is,' she said, 'that as I haven't got a number plate they can't identify me. All I've got to do is give them the slip.'

'For God's sake, Val, this isn't a car chase in a film! Anyway you can't outrun them in this old thing!'

'You'll see. I tell you, she can *fly*!' And she stepped on it.

Now off the high road they were in a maze of identical back streets, narrow, with cars parked on both sides and only just room for one car to get through. Then up ahead traffic lights appeared. Green. OK. Then amber. The Mini wasn't there yet but the taxi in front drew up just as the light turned to red. Val swung the car out and round it into the crossroads as another car from their left, just setting off on its green light, tipped to a sudden screeching halt to avoid hitting them amidships.

'Nice work,' Val congratulated herself, for the police car, though other drivers held back for it, took the crossroads with greater caution and so lost some ground. 'Right, now get ready for the great disappearing act.'

'What?'

'Hang on!'

With a fumbling at the dashboard Val switched off the lights and with another sudden wrench of the wheel she whipped the car across the road in the face of oncoming traffic into a narrow side street. Munster Close was the sign Johnny saw. Right, this was it, the end of the road either way: either their little car would have given the police the slip or the authorities would have them in a cul-de-sac and that would be that. And God knew what consequences for Val. She tucked the car into a gap by the kerb a little way into the close, switched off the engine and slumped in her seat.

Success! The police car sped past and away, sirens blaring. Val was cock-a-hoop. 'Ha, ha! Who says this isn't like a car chase in a film! So much for the fuzz. Right, let's get out of here.'

'Val, we've got to –'

But Val was revving and going.

'Just a victory roll round here and we're off – back to freedom!'

Johnny never knew whether Val spotted the speed bump or whether in her triumph she ignored the danger it posed to the little old car, but careering into it the Mini virtually took off – hadn't Val said 'This thing can fly!'? – seemed suspended a long contemplative moment in mid-air, then came down with a hideous metallic crash as if, without the benefit of rubber tyres or a suspension system, it had been dropped from a considerable height directly on to its undercarriage.

The police car, cruising now silently into the close like a shark sure of its prey, overtook smartly and turned round to face the elusive red Mini and so prevent its escape. The two officers in the front had to laugh at the sight before them: a car with its wheels spread outwards at an angle like a giraffe's legs at a water hole.

Val's driving days were over.

It was several months later, when he was well clear of London and Outram Park, that Johnny received the following letter, forwarded (eventually) by Angus. There was no address or date but it had a French stamp.

'Dear Johnny, I never write letters and I never say sorry but I did feel bad about our row over the car.' Johnny didn't remember a row exactly – he just remembered being unilaterally shouted at, Val spewing her class hatred and mindless calls for 'revolution'. She was wrong about Rawle but maybe, he had since wondered, maybe she wasn't entirely wrong about him.

Maybe he was useless in a place like Outram Park. 'I guess the police rather took my mind off you and I don't blame you bringing our relationship to an end by disappearing off for the holidays like you did. I hope you're OK.

Anyway I thought you might like to know what happened afterwards. It went to court of course which is ridiculous when you think of the criminality of the entire capitalist system but there I was for the hearing and you'll never guess who the magistrate was – Half-Baker! taking time off from not running Outram Park to ponce about in a wig judging innocent people like me. (He wasn't really wearing a wig.) Well, he couldn't hear the case for obvious reasons but as headmaster he was absolutely not pleased about my brush with the law which I'd carefully kept quiet about at school. It wasn't a sacking offence but he got really frosty with me and when he started talking about "setting an example to the young" I thought Well, sod it, what am I doing here? I've done three and a half years at the old place and that's enough. It might have been different if Eddy'd still been there but there were other things going on nothing to do with school and that's why I'm here now. Not working of course and so what with a big fine on top of it all I'm broke and forced to spend time in my room writing letters to old boyfriends because I can't afford to go out! But the spirit of revolution is really strong here in Paris, much stronger than in London so I'm posing as a post-graduate exchange student if anyone asks me, and helping the cause. There's a terrific atmosphere. I think there might be some really interesting things happening here before long. Come and join us!

Actually I wanted to thank you for some good times. If you ever want a reference as a lover I'm your girl!! On second thoughts <u>not</u> – because I might want to come back and marry you so don't give yourself away! We have differences of opinion about things but don't we make a great couple? Anyway, who says marriage should be peaceful? In fact I think it would be much better with a bit of fighting! Also I'll want a baby (or two, or three…) one day – you'd make a great dad!

Don't worry – only joking.

XXX V.

P.S. Or am I?'

5

TALBOT COLLEGE 3

'What's your opinion then, of this comprehensive experiment?' asked the headmaster.

'That it's still at an experimental stage.'

'And did you enjoy being part of that experiment?'

'Not enough to carry on working in the laboratory. I felt like a zoo keeper expected to mind the penguins and the panthers and all the rest of the animals in the same run.'

'And not just minding them, like Noah, but training them for the circus at the same time?'

'Yes, I'd rather have the panthers over there and deal with them on their own in a manner suited to panthers.'

'But the social argument – or should I say the social*ist* argument?' – the headmaster smiled – 'is that they're animals first and species second. Classification – taking the word literally – is anathema. "All animals are equal." '

'They may be equal but they're not the same.'

'But they are capable of change, of progress. If you treat penguins only as penguins then how can they become panthers? Comprehensivisation – heavens, what a word! – is about species mobility. Nobody should be condemned at age eleven to being a brickie if he has the capacity to become a brain surgeon.'

'That's the ideal behind it, I see that, but that's to force a social aim upon an educational purpose, which is wrong in my opinion. My preference is for teaching rather than social work.'

'Very well. But education doesn't take place outside society – it is not a monastic proceeding. So what is your educational vision? You young people nowadays seem to have "vision" – the days of the old pragmatists like me are over, it seems. Or, to revert to our earlier question, how do we inspire the young with a love of learning – in other words give them a true education

– while at the same time fitting them for a useful role in society as we have it?'

' "Society as we have it" – aye, there's the rub. Some people believe we should change society by means of education rather than make education serve society as we have it.'

'But you don't?'

'No. But I believe there is scope for educational idealism that will improve society. Surely there's always scope for improving society.'

'Improving rather than changing?'

'Yes.'

'A philosopher would consider that a purely subjective distinction.'

'I'm not a philosopher.'

The headmaster seemed to be reflecting on something. 'Mr Clarke,' he said, 'since we're talking of society what would you feel about being master-in-charge of the Talbot College "Crossbenchers", the politics society? I think you'd make a rather good job of it.'

6

CLOUDS

If you want to make God laugh tell him your plans.
(R.D.Laing)

Dear Onjon and Fi,
I decided to write a diary of my time here. Then I thought you might like to know something of what I'm doing and as I won't be able to come to Rawle this term I thought why not combine my diary with a letter to you? A lot of it'll probably be more than you want to know but you can ignore that and I can relieve you of the diary-letters later for my own interest afterwards. OK? Here goes.

April 21 The Day Book

At the end of each day the children hand in their Day Books. The Day Book is a foolscap exercise book with hard green covers. The front cover has printed on it – well, embossed in gold actually – the Clouds pentangle. The five points of this star are Faith, Fire, Fellowship, Fancy and Freedom. These are the principles of the school and date from the end of the nineteenth century when the founding headmaster, Edward Masterson, started the place. (The children call these the Five Farts.)

In the inside front cover of the Day Book the pupil puts his or her personal details: name (in full), age, tutor's name, dormitory, blood group, star sign (honestly) etc. The name is cauterised, branded, into the front cover above the pentangle, because this is a boy or girl's main possession. It must not be lost.

In the inside back cover is the 'Sphere'. Of course being in a book it can have only two dimensions but it should be thought of as a ball not just a circle or ring. In the centre is 'I' and round the outside like a casing is 'God'. Between those two is all the other things, Principle, Strategy and Tactics, in three concentric rings. The 'I' is divided into four parts, Brain and Body, Soul and Society. Each of these is divided into two, so for example, Brain is in two parts: Imagination and Intellect. The outer ring is what you might call explanatory detail, so for example under The World, which is one half of the principle Society, is Charity, Politics and Social Work.

This Masterson, the school's founder, intended his Sphere to cover all aspects of humanity. Live by those principles and you are a full and rounded person. If everyone lived this full life the world would be an excellent place, though how anyone could possibly find time for it all beats me. Anyway, that is the Clouds vision. Talk about a rounded education!

This Sphere is supported by a far more detailed statement of how all these tactics are to be put into practice. Talking of practice, for example, it is laid down how many minutes a day you should spend on your musical instrument, and also what time of day that should be. It is also decreed at what hour you should visit 'the closet' and which direction you should face while engaged there, though you'd think that would be predetermined by the orientation of the loo itself! Well, those are just two examples of what this Masterson fellow originally dreamed up for his 'new school' but as they now read a bit daftly in the modern age no one pays any attention to them. But what a regime! It makes the monastic life seem like a holiday camp in comparison!

To return to the Day Book, here is the routine at the end of every day. More like a ritual really. It's called Evening Gathering, time 8.30. The children line up outside the Hall (there isn't a chapel) and solemnly file in, youngest first, by tutor group to present their books. The staff are lurking at the back looking bored but quite glad they don't have to do anything for once. The Hed – yes, spelt like that because Masterson had a thing about phonetic spelling and changed all sorts of words in school (including 'skool', like Molesworth!) but this is the only one that's stuck – the Hed is sitting at the Table in the Chair, behind him on the panelled wall picked out in gold paint is the Clouds pentangle, man-size. So the children file past and place their books on the Table in a tutor group pile, shaking the Hed by the hand as they do so in a sort of reverse speech day action. The Hed says, 'Thank you, Tanya, thank you, Evan,' and so on. The only variation in this is if there's a Special, i.e. a child whose progress is under scrutiny for some reason. Then the Hed might take a quick look and maybe have a word, nothing much as there are another 163 children still to go.

Then when the whole lot are in and everyone's sat down the Hed makes a few comments about the day, reads some improving passage of philosophy or poetry and then the staff make their own announcements about what they're offering the following day so that the children can have a think overnight about which of those things they fancy doing – because there is no set timetable!

The children then file out and the staff get down to the job of reading the books of the children in their tutor group. This takes a while, some of them are quite detailed and some hard to read! Then there is general discussion about the Specials – Angeline, say, who seems reluctant to do anything involving figures. Can anyone report any progress on that front today? Any suggestions for a new way of encouraging her? Is it a case for the educational psychologist, or perhaps the school counsellor as the problem may be more emotional than cognitive. How is she getting on with her peer group? Are there problems at home? (The school counsellor – Josie who has a crewcut – is a semi-trained member of staff who listens to the children's private woes on a confessional basis, like a priest. NB just as there is no chapel so there is no chaplain.)

After the Specials the tutors take it in turns to bring up any new issues that might have arisen during the day and the Hed winds up the meeting with some words of wisdom and encouragement to his jaded staff who can't get home fast enough. By now it's 9.30 or later but this is not the end of it for the Hed. Incredible though it may seem, he then settles down to all the books and reads through each one and then makes a written comment at the bottom of the page so that when the children get their books back at Morning Gathering twelve hours later they will find something like, 'Please show me that animal mask you did in Art. What will you do next? M.A.' (that's the Hed's initials, Menzies – pron. 'Mingies' – Arkwright). Think of the time that takes – apparently he sometimes writes reams – but allegedly he doesn't sleep anyway. More about him soon.

Morning Gathering: books back, more improving readings or some music, more staff announcements. Then Tutor Group meeting at which the children write down their plan for the day, discussing it with their tutor and each other if they are so inclined.

Believe it or not there's another Gathering in the day but that's really just an extension of lunch and consists of more staff announcements, like 'Farm Group, meet at Stott's Barn 2.30 – wellies must be worn,' or 'Crystallography Club is for T.G.'s 1-3 only. Meet in the junior science lab at 4. There's a film so don't be late.' That sort of thing. Usually Matron has most to say and everyone groans when she gets to her feet but in quite a friendly way because the children know she does actually care for them even if she thinks nose-drops are a cure-all. 'I've got this painful elbow, Mrs Fawkus.'

'Right, sit down, put your head back.'

April 22 Menzies Arkwright

The first time I came to Clouds was when I was in the sixth form at Worthington. It was a daytrip to play a game of cricket. (There's no cricket at Clouds now.) The reason for the visit was that the then headmaster, Mr Kendall, had been on the staff at Worthington and he'd invited us to make the journey over. Come to think of it, it wasn't a daytrip, it was an overnight visit because my most vivid memory was of the Friday Night Social, as it was called, the night before, when I found myself on the cliffs looking out on to the Solent and kissing a girl I'd only just met called Annabel – or, rather, she was kissing me, but that's another story.

The point is I thought why not try Mr Kendall for a job for the summer term as part of my exploration of English education? It would make a good contrast to Outram Park, not to mention Eaton House. Well, he wrote back to me saying he was now retired but he would refer my application to the new headmaster with a good reference which was kind of him considering he didn't know me very well. And this Menzies Arkwright took me on even though there wasn't exactly a vacancy for an English teacher. 'I'm not appointing an English teacher,' he said. 'I'm appointing Johnny Clarke,' which seemed very nice at the time, and gives you an idea of the unusual man he is.

M.A. is all for trying things, which is fine, though it does mean we (the staff) have to be prepared to try things too. 'All education is experimental', he says. This doesn't suit all staff because teachers tend not to be good explorers or learners, I've discovered, which is odd. They like to know where they are and to be in charge, not to be risking their dignity or authority by branching out or put to any test which as I say is odd when you think how much time they spend testing others. I rather like it but then I'm lucky enough not to be old and set in my ways and anyway I've got nothing to lose having no dignity to start with, whereas the staff here have mostly been here quite a long time and have families and pensions to think about. Obviously M.A. is changing things and they are nervous about that. They are like limpets that have acquired their own safe little places on the rock and there they stick. Now the tide's gone out – i.e. M.A. is exposing them to some new conditions and making new demands – and they're just hanging on, counting on the tide coming in again before long to cover them up comfortably once more. Some of them have seen several Heds come and go and so they take a lofty and relaxed attitude to it all but some as I say are nervous.

There are a lot of things said about M.A. and a lot of different rumours and opinions but the basic facts are that he is a young man – barely thirty – and he's a New Zealander. You might not think of New Zealand as a fount of educational revolution but he has brought with him a strong conviction about how a school should work and he is clearly determined to do his utmost to put this conviction into practice as far as lies within his power. And his power is very considerable – not just in the way that any headmaster's is but with plenty on top. Rumour has it that when Mr Kendall left Clouds the school was in a bad way financially. There'd been some building work – a new art block, for example – but a drop in pupil numbers that put the school into heavy debt. The members of the Conclave (Clouds term for governing body) were on the point of closing the school but then along came this whizz-kid from downunder who was a passionate believer in the Clouds principles and had bags of energy to back it up. This powerful conviction was enough for Conclave, who were staring into the abyss of the closure of the oldest 'progressive' school in the country. Obviously he was a big gamble but as an alternative to packing up he was an acceptable choice. So they took him on and he took on Clouds on the understanding that he must be given a free hand. He would do whatever he wanted and judged to be the way to get Clouds back in business. Fortunately one thing he and Conclave agreed on was that a return to fundamentals was necessary for a return to solvency, not down to all that detail about practice times and 'evacuation' procedures and phonetic spelling but the basics, the essence of the Sphere. For Mr Kendall, it seems, had allowed the school to drift away from some of its original principles and to become more like an ordinary public school with a set timetable, team sports and so on. On that basis, it wasn't going to succeed, not in competition with places like Worthington not far away, being rather small with limited facilities and in an odd sort of place, i.e. perched on a cliff on the Isle of Wight. The Conclave decided that it was M.A. or bust so in he came, abolished the timetable as such, ploughed up the cricket field and planted it with potatoes. Competition he saw as something inevitable given human nature but not as something to be encouraged. Cricket, anyway, was a complete waste of time and resources, in his view. Planting potatoes, watching them grow, harvesting and then eating them made 'the young aware of their relationship to and dependence upon the land, deepening their understanding of the practical realities of life.'(M.A.) Next came the sheep.

April 24 My Tutor Group

Talking of sheep…! All the tutor groups (which is just a posh word for 'form') have names drawn from the flora – Heather, Bracken, Rowan, Bramble etc. Mine is called Ash, or Trash by the staff in private on account of the low calibre of its members. Well, thanks! Their usual tutor, Bernard Someone, has gone on a term's sabbatical to some school in Germany run on similar lines and I have the pleasure of seeing them through to the end of what is normally called the academic year except the word 'academic' is not used here. At the moment they don't think much of me, my group, and I'm finding it hard to think much of them. They are stodgy and sullen and their response to all the opportunities and stimulants and challenges presented them on the educational menu here is to groan softly and occupy themselves (if with anything) with trivial concerns of their own. Tom, for example.

Tom is goodness knows how old but surely more than the fourteen he is supposed to be. He is tall(er than me), spotty, slack-jawed and with a vacant air, his eyes glazed. He enters the tutor room as if he just happened to be passing and thought he might as well look in, having nothing more pressing to do. Keeping him and his Day Book connected is a constant battle and he never has anything to write with. I said, 'Tom, suppose you were a plumber. Would you turn up for a job without your bag of tools?' 'No.' 'Right, well, you're a student and a student's tools are his reading and writing materials, you can't do anything without them.' Dim as he is I think he got the point – it just hasn't made any difference, the reason being that he doesn't see himself as a student – it's not something he *wants* to be. When a pen is required one of the girls (who usually have armfuls of writing implements) virtually compete to provide him with one. In so far as he has any positive instincts they consist of chatting to the girls (he's good at that) and sport. Formal sport has been virtually abolished under M.A.'s regime which is tough on Tom as there are no (official) games or coaching or school matches to liven up school life. Actually, on second thoughts, maybe that isn't such a bad thing as it means he has to do the organising.

(Sport hasn't been banned, it's just not catered for any more.) When he does settle to anything it is to looking over the list of names he has on a piece of scruffy paper he keeps in his back pocket. This is the football teams (although it's the summer term) and he and Sebastian and Rupert can spend any amount of time going over this list and shaping the league and order of play etc. for that day's games. So really it is unintentionally quite educational in the Clouds sense. The sports fields may have been ploughed up but that doesn't stop the boys from finding places to play.

So that's Tom. Now for a girl or two.

Stella – Stell to her friends! – returned late for the start of term because she was on holiday in some exotic location and I really haven't got the measure of her at all. She is small, dark and thoroughly tanned from her time in Barbados or Zermatt or wherever it was, and very fidgety as if there were something itching her inside. Maybe it's her hormones. She is certainly 'into boys', as I could tell from a little notebook she left behind the other day. It had a heading 'Boys I've been out with' and that had half a dozen names to it, and then alongside that 'Boys I want to go out with', with the names of another handful of potential victims. I'm not quite sure what 'go out with' means in the Clouds context as there is no going out allowed but I have a feeling it may be more than holding hands behind the bike shed. She's not old enough to attend the Friday Night Socials. Anyway she's got a look about her and I shouldn't be surprised if she soon twigs that getting on in life in her case is going to be due to assets other than her brain! She does very little work, or indeed anything and her Day Book is more blank space than anything else. Oddly, though, she does at moments step aside from her boy obsession and show signs of wanting to get on. I picture a highly successful father behind her who wants his daughter to succeed when all she wants to do is to wallow in the pleasures her father's success has provided for her, viz. having fun with boys on palm-fringed beaches or sun-kissed ski slopes. She can manage occasional bursts of huge concentration but with meagre results, like a dog enthusiastically digging a pointless hole in the sand. This

I fear she will use as an excuse for bothering less in the future. She will say, 'I did try, really I did, but look where it got me – nowhere!' She likes to get things right but I'm afraid she isn't often going to.

Then there's Anna-one (there are two). She is tall, rather stand-offish and as dim as Tom and would be a suitable case for Val as she is clearly what is called 'dyslexic'. I mean she literally cannot read. When we are reading round the class (I take them for English as well as being their tutor) she will often volunteer eagerly, launch into it, as often as not in the wrong place and quickly founder with 'Oh, I can't do it!' and wave her arms in the air and drop her head on to the desk in a dramatic manner which everyone ignores (they're used to it) except me who tries to be terribly understanding and patient and quietly encouraging to absolutely no effect as Anna is immoveable. It's odd, she looks attentive much of the time but then something she says or does make you realise she's miles away and has taken nothing in. Poor Anna-one, like Stella she wants to get on but the grim fact is she hasn't got the mental equipment needed, and there doesn't seem to be anything else on her side (unlike Stell with her looks).

Actually they all seem oddly unimpressionable, come to think of it. Sometimes I feel as if I might as well not be there, they live in a world of their own, like Anna-one who doesn't seem to relate to the others (girl or boy) at all except occasionally to carp or squabble, and like Tom and his football, or Stella and her love life.

They don't seem to exist as a group at all or to have any sense of themselves as pupils. As you can see I am not very optimistic about bringing this lot to life. Any ideas?!

April 27 My Room

You should see my bothy! That's what it's called. The house here was originally built for some rich industrialist at the turn of the century (before it became a lunatic asylum before it became a TB hospital before it became a school!) and the bothy was the name for the summerhouse he had built to entertain his family or friends or mistress or old mum or whatever fantasy you subscribe to. Its special feature is that it was built to revolve so that those inside could get a change of outlook and no doubt catch the sun as it moved round. Clever. Unfortunately the works are long since rusted up but it nonetheless has a wonderful position on the side of the little valley called the Dell that runs down from the school and its grounds at the top of the cliff to the virtually private beach at the bottom. It has terrific views out over the Solent to the coast and east out over the Channel and it gets sun virtually all day.

Imagine something that's a large-scale cross between a garden shed, a cabin-in-the-woods and a sports pavilion, with a verandah that runs round three sides and where perhaps the TB sufferers lay out in their beds in the sunshine. It has no electricity and no running water except in the tiny stream that runs down through the Dell to the sea. Its last incarnation was as an art school which is why (I guess) some roof lights have been put in the north side so that some of the glare from the east and the south sides could be softened a bit for artistic purposes. The posh new modern art school that rendered the school almost bankrupt then made the bothy redundant and it was locked up, to become the haunt of smokers and snoggers getting out of sight of school until one day some fanciful soul alleged she had seen a strange man behaving strangely and a strange light! This made the place both spooky and dangerous so that it was avoided until M.A. had the bright idea of turning it into bachelor accommodation – hence me.

It is the most wonderful place I have ever called home, entirely private – I have it all to myself and it is overlooked by nothing except the wind-bent sycamores behind. The working day ends late (as I have explained) but what with the open sky and the time of year it is still virtually daylight when I get down here. I get water from the stream to do my teeth, pee in the gorse (anything more serious has to be done in the big house!) and go to bed by the remains of natural light or I light the candle and I have a torch 'in case'. It has bare boards and there's just a bed but plenty of built-in cupboards for my stuff and I've been given a sort-of desk. It's not always very warm but I sleep like a log though I wake early because the old blinds from the art school days are hardly a substitute for curtains and there are so many windows. I can lie in bed and look out over the sea into the eye of the rising sun. The big ships, liners and tankers and naval vessels, are coming in and going out on the tide past the Martello towers and it's all utterly quiet except, of course, for the dawn chorus which is deafening! Doesn't it sound wonderful?

And all that is something of a contrast to my tutor room where most of the rest of my time is spent. It is small but high, it has only one window which is hard to open and which comes down (it's a sash window) like a guillotine unless you prop it open and it looks out on the kitchen yard which can be noisy with clattering milk crates and suchlike, as well as being somewhat dank and enclosed. Why does dismal red brick overshadow my life?! Eaton House, Outram Park and now Clouds (or Monkstone Hall as it was apparently once called, named after the nearby village).

Anyway that isn't the worst of my tutor room. The worst is the desks. I really wonder where they can have come from – unless they were bought new in 1887! I think they were made out of battleships, both the old wooden Victory-type things and the ironclads because the tops of these double things are of very thick and sturdy wood. Actually they're not as solid as they were because generations of children have gouged and etched and bored into them so that they are completely hopeless for writing on without something thick under your paper. You might see E.H. carved a quarter of an inch deep into the top, the letters two inches high, quite neat work some of it, surprisingly, but also there are random excavations of a more casual nature, in one or two instances holes, or craters even, having been laboriously bored over perhaps many years by many hands right through these mighty planks. What on earth, I wonder, was the master in charge doing while the boys were carving away like that? How could you not notice someone doing something like that? Some of the work is on such a scale you'd think you'd need a hammer and chisel to do it!

These surfaces are connected to the bench and its back by

two enormous curved steel struts that are shiny with the scuffing of thousands of shoes (or boots as they would originally have been). And these things are virtually immoveable. I tried but got nowhere on my own and Tom had to help me. The solid steel struts were so hefty that they ripped splinters out of the floorboards and snagged on the polished nail-heads sticking up through them. So I'm stuck with those horrible, immoveable dreadnoughts, occupied by those horrible, immoveable teenagers. Help!

April 29 Minkie's Educational Philosophy

I had a really good talk with Minkie yesterday. It was all about education so maybe you won't find it very interesting but I'd like to set it down anyway for the record.

We were in his flat which is a garret right up in the roof of the main building – not very grand for a headmaster, even a bachelor, but he isn't bothered about that sort of thing. It's very sparsely furnished as if he really hadn't got time for material things at all. He doesn't sleep (much), doesn't eat (much), looks as thin and pale as a ghost – it's a wonder he's alive at all: I think he lives on air – and argument and conviction – like an Old Testament prophet!

'What do you understand?' he asked me, 'by a progressive school?'

'Well, the popular idea is of a place where the children let it all hang out, doing their own thing –'

'– calling the staff by their first names, smoking pot and sleeping together. Yes, I know what the popular idea is and no doubt there's a fair amount of truth in that. But what I asked you was what you understood by it.'

'Progressive means going forward,' says I, resorting to my classical education to play for time.

'And is it forward-going to encourage children to go backwards?'

'By definition not.'

'And yet this popular idea of progressive is actually regressive.'

'Er, how's that?'

'Do you believe that children should be encouraged to think that they're entitled to the Garden of Eden, to be stress-free, to do just what they want?'

'No, that's not preparing them for life.'

'Indeed it isn't. It's a childish fantasy – the infant totally self-absorbed, wailing and sulking if it doesn't get what it wants.'

'I see what you mean by regressive then.'

'This approach is touted as giving the children freedom – but it isn't freedom, it's licence.'

'Which means self-indulgence.'

'Yes – and the consequences are?'

'Failure to grow up?'

'Worse than that. Give a kid the run of the sweetie shop and what do you get?'

'A happy kid.'

'For the first half hour of guzzling. Then what?'

'A vomiting kid.'

'Exactly – surfeit, nausea. He thought he was in heaven and so he was at first but then pretty soon he's feeling awful – big disappointment. And what follows from disappointment?'

'Bitterness?'

'Bitterness, envy, indifference, self-centredness, irrationality, cruelty – violence to self and others.'

This was strong stuff, you can appreciate. I was getting a hefty Socratic going-over with a big dollop of some new morality I hadn't got the hang of. We seemed to have gone from too many Mars bars to suicide and murder in a sentence and I was struggling to keep up.

'Now what does today's fashionable counterculture preach?' he asked.

'Counterculture?' I queried. (Nothing to do with running a shop, that was for sure!)

'The anti-scientific materialism position.'

'Ah, well that says the world is in thrall to technology and consumerism – we're gobbling up the world's finite resources, the rich get richer, the poor get poorer etc.'

'Quite. "The yelping and carnivorous crowd, tearing

each other to pieces," as Ruskin has it. And what do the counterculturalists say we should do?'

'Wear flowers in our hair and make love not war.'

'Exactly, so that the world will become a beautiful place again, restored to its primal state of harmony.'

'Back to the Garden of Eden.'

'Right again. But like it or not, Planet Earth is not the Garden of Eden. Flowers might blossom here without man's help but where's the potato crop coming from? After you've made love what do you get for supper?'

'So if it's true that we consumers are ruining the world by littering it with broken-down fridges but also true that we need to make a living, to work, then we need to get some sort of balance.'

'Precisely. And getting that balance is what we educationalists have to aim for. So if progressive means anything it means restoring the balance between flowers and fridges.'

Here follows Minkie's platonic myth of the caveman:

'He stands outside his home watching the sun set over the plain where the mammoth roam. Behind him his woman is cooking his scanty supper, the last of their supplies. Does he say to her, "Hey, look at the lovely sunset, get that effect of the light falling on the autumn foliage?" Or is he preparing in his mind the next day's hunt on the success of which depends his ability to feed his wife and child?'

'Well, your flower power man is all for admiring the sunset while your scientific materialist is all for hunting tactics.'

'Exactly. So what the Clouds caveman (as it were) does is have a good think about the mammoth job and perhaps discuss it with his neighbours – that's Fellowship – and after supper he'll go back into the cave and paint or carve on the wall pictures of the hunt – that's Fancy, the artistic response which is as natural and necessary to man as sex and hunger. Contemplation and planning will have filled him with Fire – the urge to action – and he will arise the next morning inspired by Faith in his own and his fellows' ability and in the world he has inherited, a place which is both beautiful and useful. It feeds his body and it feeds his soul.'

'And what then is the Freedom?' I ask.

'His freedom lies in the fact that he is not an ant, he does not live an entirely instinctual and unreflective existence. He can choose to come and go, hunt or weave, walk or run, sing or dance. The pelt with which he covers himself at night is the fruit of his labour and skill in killing the animal it belonged to and of his woman's in curing it for human use. His freedom consists then in making choices, in exercising his skills, in providing for himself and celebrating the whole process.'

'Right, that's the balance,' I say, 'but balance of what exactly? What's in the scales?'

'What's in the scales is plenty – richness and variety. These must invigorate our children with the true freedom of participation, of enjoyment – in reason and the imagination, in art and nature, words and numbers, the library and the hay-field, the sea and the forest – and the more the better, and the deeper and wider the better.'

'The teacher's job then is to arrange for this participation –'

'– to stimulate and to challenge, to present facts and invite fancies, to instruct and inspire, encourage and exhort. The soul and the mind are naturally as hungry as the body; a good school is the feeder, providing a rich and balanced diet. That way the children develop into skilled and positive individuals co-operating to create a harmonious and productive society.'

Phew! Here endeth the gospel according to Minkie as recalled by his faithful disciple, Johnny Clarke! I feel now as if I really know what I'm trying to do.

Now I am proud to tell you that I composed the above between five and six this morning, inspired by the dawn, a brilliant white dawn with a huge sun, plus another element, namely Minkie himself, on the beach. His being there was no great surprise because a) he is well known to be an early riser (in addition to being a late bedder: I told you he doesn't sleep), and b) he is a great swimmer, an Olympic for New Zealand apparently. Anyway he'd obviously been for a swim (must have been freezing) because his black hair was wet and he was rubbing himself down with a towel. After that he got dressed right out in the open though at the end of the beach by some rocks where he had parked his clothes and towel. I say 'clothes' but somehow the word 'garments' seems more apt because they consisted of some sort of oriental robes or pyjamas, goldy-yellow in colour, and he was doing something unusual, that is to say, some sort of exercises, not your old-fashioned PE like we did at school but maybe more like yoga, or one of those oriental meditation practices because the movements he was making were not the sort of 'hup-two-three-hup' kind of thing but more like postures, stretching forward, for example, one knee bent, the other leg behind, his arms doing calculated movements in the air with the action of slowly cutting with the hand on edge or turning the palm up to the sun which he was facing throughout these quite lengthy exercises. One of the things he did for a while was to sit cross-legged with his hands, palms upwards, resting on his knees. He was like that, quite still, for several minutes.

There was something a bit odd about it all, no wonder there are rumours about him, but I stopped watching after a while then kept my head down because he would have come up the path past my bothy and I didn't want him to think I'd been observing him (though he wasn't making any attempt to hide).

Anyway, thanks, Fi, for helping me to think about the classroom problem. As you say, 'Classroom awful – bothy great' and there must be some way of squaring that circle. I will use my Freedom of thought, trust to the creative power of Fancy backed up by my Faith in my situation and the Fire of necessity – thank you for the Fellowship!

P.S. Great to hear of the orchard looking so fine with its blossom. Wish I could see it.

May 2 Crisis!

Yesterday I flipped! – lost my cool, blew my top, behaved in a highly unprofessional even childish manner. And do you know what? It did the trick!

It started with May morning, one of the Clouds traditions. (Funny thing – this 'progressive' school has more traditions than a 'traditional' school!) The whole school gets up before dawn and traipses down the Dell to the beach. It's a lovely beach, public of course as all beaches are but enclosed at either end by promontories of rocks. At high tide this means the beach is inaccessible from the seashore except by taking an awkward footpath through the trees on the cliffs above. That in turn means that it is virtually the school's private beach, certainly at this time of day. Anyway the purpose of this visit is to watch the sun rise. Perhaps that's what Minkie was doing down there the other morning – praying to the sun god to ensure a fair May morning! Well, if so his prayers were not answered because it was a thoroughly dull morning with grey cloud and a rather chilly drizzle (as it invariably is at Oxford on this occasion, as I recall).

This 'rich' experience the children responded to with characteristic indifference, huddled under anoraks, the sleep still in their eyes with the exception of some of the younger ones who mucked about and pushed each other over. The last thing they were aware of was this being the morning that celebrates (in a calendar rather than solstitial way) the final triumph of light over darkness, the new over the old, and the natural law of renewal, witness the blackbirds singing away in the trees, the gulls frolicking overhead as they prepared their nesting sites and geared themselves up for a long summer of procreation, responsible parenting, foraging for food etc., as Minkie attempted to explain to the assembled pupils, his words settling like droplets of drizzle upon their hunched shoulders.

Later at Morning Gathering he gave them a bit of a talking-to along the lines of the need to unleash their inner energies so that they made the most of time and life for both were precious. (I guess he was a bit disappointed with their response to the dawn thing.) He explained how each one of them was a unique creation, the only survivor of millions of spermatozoa that had perished on the way through the appropriate tubes, swimming in a dense shoal of tiny particles, all of whom, bar ONE, failed at or before the last fence, leaving 'You, Elizabeth, you, Ben…' and the whole lot of them as the single victor in this mass race to breast the tape of conception. Each one of them was a billion-to-one chance of survival – and they'd made it! How lucky they were to be alive, how uniquely privileged! How could they bring themselves to waste a single moment blah blah.

The children responded with their customary stolidity. There was the odd smirk at the mention of spermatozoa but otherwise expressions of indifference tinged faintly with distaste. Being the lucky winner in a life-and-death sperm race was not an image of themselves any of the children seemed eager to embrace. In fact they all looked as if they'd rather go back to bed.

Then it was tutor time. In preparation for the day (and before Minkie's two contributions) I had typed out and cyclostyled some stuff appropriate to the time of year, not your 'Corinna's gone a-maying, with a hey, nonny no,' sort of thing but some excerpts from prose as well as verse that made up a celebration of spring and natural beauty generally. I got a bit carried away and the resulting product was almost a booklet, I was really proud of it and started having fantasies about producing an anthology of my own for use in schools.

So when I put this precious baby of mine out before them I did so with what I now realise was a volatile mixture of pride, hope, excitement and, on the other side of the scales, an accumulated annoyance at a) all the indifference they had shown hitherto which I had met with cheerful patience, and b) Minkie's performance both on the beach and at Morning Gathering, a performance that was stirring the suspicion in my mind that while he had a jolly good notion of education (see my last) he himself was maybe not all that good at making it happen. He hadn't exactly lectured them and told them boring schoolmasterly things about the need to make the most of their opportunities and all that rot but his way of putting it amounted to the same thing and was equally ineffective.

Thus, as you can appreciate, I was in a pretty wrought-up state by the time the group strolled in and took their customary seats. (The trouble with double desks is that you either have two friends getting too close together for the good of their work – Tom and Rupert, for example, or Lily and Freda – or two people who don't like one another getting closer than they want, or someone taking up the space for two because either they refuse to sit with anyone else or because no one else will sit with them, Anna-one, for example.)

Right, so there we are, I have distributed my precious offering and invited everyone to give it their attention. 'We will read the pieces round,' I say, 'then talk about them.' Lily reluctantly mumbles through 'The Darkling Thrush', Freda murders Dorothy Wordsworth's little prose appreciation of the celandine. Well, no worse than can be expected, I suppose. 'Right, Tom, the Edward Thomas, please.' 'Unhh?' 'The Edward Thomas poem. "Adlestrop", third one down.' Clumsily he shuffles some other paper from off the worksheet and I see, going up to him, what it is. It's his bloody football list, of course! I see red. I slam my hand down on it and scrumple the wretched thing up in an enraged fist. Bang! Scrunch! '*Right*,' I say, 'it is clear that what we are doing is a complete waste of time.' Then for the first time since I met them I have their attention, they are looking up at me, albeit like cows unsure whether this sudden intruder is really a menace or can be safely ignored. 'A complete...waste... of time,' I repeat ostensibly for emphasis though actually uncertain what to do next, having surprised myself more than them probably with my outburst. I stride about collecting up my precious products from in front of their bemused faces. 'You are clearly not...' but I don't know how to continue. Where do I go from here? I don't know. So what do I do? I march out of the room!

And come down here, to my retreat, my bothy. What am I doing, I ask myself. I must be mad. What will Minkie say? What will he think when he sees in their Day Books, 'Mr C walked out in a rage. We did not know what we had done wrong and we did not know what we should do.'? They'd be sure to make the most of it. This is grossly irresponsible on my part – you can't just abandon a class. Whatever they do or say you must be there, you must supervise them even if you've lost control. I pace up and down my room. What should I do? Should I go back to the group and try and pick up from where I left off? Perhaps my outburst has woken them up and we might get some sort of work done. Maybe this'll be a turning point – if they're still there, that is. On the other hand maybe I should just pack my bag and catch the next ferry out of Ryde. There's something about this place – or is it something about me? – that just isn't working properly.

Then I hear a little rap on my door. It's Robbie. I don't think I've told you about Robbie. Funny, because in some ways he's the worst of the lot. That is, he's one of those who's simply unschoolable. He's not rebellious or bloody-minded, or prone to outbursts of temper or a kleptomaniac or a liar or anything dramatic like that; he's just never where he should be, never conforms to any expectation, never has the necessary books or does the work he commits himself to. He wanders round the school like a vagrant or a lost soul with an expression of bleak purposelessness, often with an open book in his hand for he reads about three books a day. He's lost a pair of shoes, he'll say, or he's just on the way somewhere from surgery or Mr S. has asked to see him. When he does do anything it is entirely in his own way and on his own terms. At the same time, paradoxically, he is hungry for praise and commendation like an anxious small child, presenting his Day Book for signature – he's a Special, of course – 'Look how much I've done.'

I open the door to Robbie. He looks unhappy.

'They want to know if you're going back,' he says.

Clever of them to nominate Robbie for the job, so naughty, so pathetic.

I reply, 'They've got a choice. Either I come back and we do some work, or … they come here.'

Why did I say that? I hadn't planned to. Inspiration? Or a fool rushing in?

Robbie departs slowly as if honourably burdened with a mighty mission. Five minutes later there is a huddle and a hubbub outside my door and there they all are, bright as buttons.

May 7 Ghost Stories

I am going to create a Little Green School Book of useful guidance for teachers. How's that for presumptuous?!

Principle 1: Do not lecture (? hector) children collectively. It is a complete waste of everybody's time and your energy and it just makes them sullen and dispirited. (Plus it is usually a substitute on the part of the hectorer for actually doing anything to solve the problem concerned.)

2: Don't think that because they are looking at you while you're talking they are listening to what you say and taking it in. They may well not be doing either but have learnt to act the part. Anyway listening actively is difficult. How many adults do it well? (How many teachers particularly?)

3. Don't bombard them with learning material. What you present as a valuable gift they receive as a burden. (The only thing children like to be bombarded with is sweets.)

4. There is no child completely out of reach or incapable of improvement.

How's that for a start?

Now here's how things have progressed since my last.

You suggested, Fi, that there might be some way of squaring off the 'awful classroom/lovely bothy' situation. Well, I think I've found it.

It's nearly a week since that moment when I walked out on the children and they turned up on my doorstep. Is it only a week? Are they really the same children! When they first arrived there was a twinkle in their eye but they also looked pretty sheepish and unsure. It was a strange place to them, they'd never been in the building before and they didn't quite know what to expect. Was this going to be a resumption of the lesson I had abandoned? Was I going to go on being cross with them? The most challenging question of all I doubt if they asked and certainly didn't answer: why had they come?

At any rate their initial uncertainty quickly passed and within minutes of their arrival people were chatting away quite freely. Anna-one in her clumsy but ingenuous way started it with 'Isn't it a bit spooky down here, Mr C.?' I made no attempt to restart my aborted lesson, which was doomed to failure for the simple reason that they were utterly bored by the subject of nature. What interest does a modern-day fourteen-year-old boy or girl have in a thrush singing in the twilight or some old woman wittering on about a little yellow flower? Not much, of course. 'Ah, but they should be taught that interest,' the traditionalist will reply. 'That's what education is for.' True but the question is How? Not by compulsorily smearing them with the stuff as if it were some health-giving ointment that's bound to do them good in the long run even if they turn up their noses at the smell of it, don't like the feel of it and can't see the point of it. Then how? Quite. Well, as Minkie said, all education is experimental, so experiment was what I would do.

The first issue was a practical one. My bothy contains a bed, a hard chair, a comfortable chair and a chest of drawers. While I was worrying about not having chairs or desks, the children (there are ten of them) disposed themselves around the place wherever they felt like after they'd had a good nose round and peered out of the windows in all directions. Stella, the little minx, bagged the armchair, as she thought for herself, but Anna-two wormed her way in behind her until Stella was sitting on her lap and both of them as comfortable as cats apparently. They instinctively avoided the bed (which luckily I had made) until I said there's room there and Lily and Freda dived for it. The hard chair they considerately left for me and otherwise sat or sprawled or lay on the floor, Chris with his back to the wall, Tom and Rupert with their backs to each other like bookends. Anna-one went straight for the most distant corner as far away as possible from everyone else and Robbie had to be different by remaining standing. Sebastian sat in open space cross-legged like a Buddha.

'Do you like sleeping here on your own, Mr C.?' asked Anna-two, taking up Anna-one's theme. She started plaiting Stella's dark locks.

'I'd be scared,' said Freda.

'Me too,' said Lily.

'Yah!' said Chris, 'the monk wouldn't come down this far.'

'How'd you know?'

'Yeah – he gets everywhere.'

I said, 'Hang on. What monk?'

'Didn't you know the school is haunted by a mad monk?'

'That's from when it was a monastery.'

I objected that the place had only been built in about 1870.

'Yes, but it was built on the site of an old monastery, it's in the foundations.'

'And that's why it's called Monkstone.'

'He was bricked in, this monk.'

'That's right. Henry VIII or someone pulled down all the monasteries and this monk got caught because he'd got locked in by the other monks for being mad.'

'Bricked in, you mean.'

'That was later.'

'Anyway he walks every night.'

'Moaning.'

'And praying aloud.'

I said, 'In your imaginations he does.'

Widespread indignation. 'No – honestly!'

'He's been seen.'

'Often.'

'Well, which one of you has seen him?' I asked.

Silence.

'Jen has seen him.'

'And Oscar.'

'I think I might have done too. Once. I had to go to the loo in the night and I was just tiptoeing down the –'

'No, don't go on, Chris, it really scares me, that story.'

'I know! Why don't we tell ghost stories!'

'As long as they're not monk stories.'

'Yeah, made-up ones.'

'We're not much good at stories.'

'Speak for yourself.'

'Well, we're not good at writing them.'

'I'm not good at writing anything.'

'Mr C. could tell us a ghost story.'

'That's right. He's an English teacher, he should be good at telling stories.'

'Can you, Mr C.?'

'Well, how about we all do it – take it in turns.'

'Good idea, just a bit at a time so you don't have to tell a whole one.'

'I'll start!' Robbie leapt in. 'Once upon a time in this old mansion in the middle of London underneath Big Ben there was –'

'How can a mansion be underneath Big Ben?'

'The same way the monastery is underneath Clouds.'

'Hunh!'

'Go on, Robbie.'

'And the man who lived in this underground mansion one evening he heard a strange scratching noise –'

'My turn!' Anna-one. 'And this scratching noise he thought gosh it must be mice and so he thought I must set some traps but …oh, I'm not playing any more!' In her distant corner she sits with her knees drawn up, her jumper stretched over them.

'My turn, my turn now.' Chris continues. 'And this scratching noise which wasn't mice at all because you wouldn't have just mice in a ghost story this scratching noise got louder and louder. What could it be? Tom.'

'Eh?'

'Your go.'

'No, me! I know what it was.' Rupert. 'It wasn't mice, oh no, and it wasn't even rats –'

'I hate rats.'

'It's spiders I can't stand.'

' – and it wasn't even spiders –'

'It couldn't have been as spiders don't scratch.'

'They might if they have fleas.'

'That's scratching <u>themselves</u>; this is about scratching at <u>bricks</u>.'

'Shut up! I'm telling. Not mice, not rats, not spiders and it wasn't an old dying burglar looking for gold, oh no! It was a man with a pick-axe and he bashed his way through the wall –'

'Bashing isn't scratching.'

'It sounds like it if it's far away. But then he popped his head out and said, "Hullo, I'm from the London Underground."' Rupert fell about with exaggerated laughter at his own brilliance. The girls didn't even deign to look at him.

End of storytelling session! Well, by then our hour was up and they had other places to go to as of course I did and that was the end of that new format tutor group. They didn't want to go. In their own ways they'd got comfortable in the bothy and were enjoying themselves. Were they learning anything? Probably not but at least they weren't bored.

Principle 5: A bored child never learns.

6: Classrooms were invented by adults for their own purposes and not to suit the children.

So now a few days on I can hardly keep them away from the place. We have all our tutor groups there plus our English sessions, not that I make any distinction between them. I did ask Minkie if that was all right, being in the bothy and he was positively enthusiastic and said he wished more staff were experimental like that. Of course he has read their Day Books and these are full of enthusiastic comments about working here and even Robbie has been less of a menace though perhaps largely because he's around the school less to irritate people. He doesn't irritate me because I leave him to his own devices, which used to be reading but is now writing his own ghost story. Of course, being Robbie, he has to go and use his large physics experiment book for the purpose and that doesn't go down well as you may imagine but we've got over that and Minkie is being very encouraging. The handwriting and the spelling are awful, not to mention the style and the plot, but it keeps him out of trouble which is what he's in all the rest of the time. I've (rashly) offered to type the story up for him which has excited him no end. This has been my excuse for urging him to give more thought to his presentation – I've got to read it! Crafty, eh?

At the children's request I have been allocated more tutor time. Prickles (that's Mr Pickles, alias the Hedgehog) who organises these things is obviously very sceptical about this miraculous conversion of (Tr)Ash to star status as Most Improved Tutor Group, eyeing me as if to say, 'You think you're a smart young blighter, don't you? Well, you wait,' and it makes me nervous, as if something is bound to go wrong. It's hard to see what at the moment as the atmosphere in the bothy is quietly positive. They all sit about in their self-chosen places 'doing their own thing', even if in some cases that isn't very much – but then it wasn't previously, they were just going through the motions, acting the part.

Of course Tom still spends hours on his bloody football but as I am not anxiously trying to make him work it doesn't bother me. In fact I have invited him to tell me about it and have been able to make some suggestions about the organisation which he welcomed. Is this education? Well, hardly in the conventional sense, but adults organise, don't they? The world needs organising, doesn't it? So let him develop his organisation skills, I say. Plus he has to articulate his thoughts to me, which must be good for him.

Someone found a book on calligraphy at the back of the cupboard left over from the bothy's days as an art school and now half of them are heads down over paper imitating different styles and I've had to buy some calligraphy pens for them to use. Bevis (in the new art school) has been very helpful. Real calligraphy is of course a challenging discipline and most of them are not up to it, but it has focussed them on their handwriting and they spend time copying things out – including some of the stuff in my rejected booklet of nature writings. Ironic, eh? They also, I think, take more trouble over their other work so it isn't just Art-and-English that is benefiting.

Anna-one has not joined in this. She sits in her corner, surrounded by books, acting the worker. The group do their Personal Work (Homework, or Prep to you and me) here now, their excuse being that it's quieter than their day-rooms and they can get more work done – I don't think! They talk a lot here but funnily enough they also seem to get things done at the same time. As for me, I try to do my own marking and preparation for other classes, hoping that my getting on with my work might encourage them to get on with theirs. I never tell them to keep quiet even though I do find their chatter quite distracting, but they sometimes tell each other to shut up! Anna-one (to return to her) varies between throwing up her hands – 'I can't do it – I can't do it!', and then when I gently offer guidance (which she asks for) she considers it only to reject it, determined to do things her own way.

Freda spends most of her time with her thumb in her mouth inside her sleeping bag. Several of them have brought cushions and blankets and suchlike to make themselves more comfortable. She doesn't do anything but just watches other people. I ask myself, Is this education? What are her parents getting for her fees? Answers: no it isn't, and not very much. But I can't bring myself to interfere and urge her to do things when she looks so simply content. I suppose a psychiatrist might say that she is catching up on a phase of her infancy that she somehow didn't get enough of at the appropriate stage and that means she can't truly move forward of her own volition (though I suppose she can be pushed), in which case the best thing is to let her catch up in her own good time. Isn't it like letting a tree put down its roots before it shoots up top? I just hope that she will come out of this compensation phase and move forward, grow up, though God knows how long that will take. She has one useful function in the group, however, does Freda. People show her things and talk to her about what they're doing. This is not because she's obviously interested but because she's not doing anything of her own and she'll look and listen even if she rarely takes her thumb out of her mouth to say anything.

Principle 7: What children feel like doing is what they should do. (For a while anyway.)

8: Just as it is no doubt true that 'You cain't hurry love' so – You cain't hurry education (or do I mean growing up?)

9: The urge to speak is stronger than the urge to listen (in most people anyway).

As you can see from all this I am not attempting to do any formal teaching with them. My famous nature writing booklets have been destapled and the backs of the pages are being used for writing or drawing on (though as I've said in one or two cases they're copying texts from them). So they're not doing any English as such. What am I doing then? Well, I stare out of the window quite a lot, looking at the changing colours of the water, the great liners and tankers and warships moving over it. Some of the children spend quite a lot of the time just staring too, the sun on the gorse flowers and the white specks of the seagulls in the sky. When it's fine, they drift outdoors and sit on the verandah or wander off a bit. They don't go far, they don't want to. No one's pulling them back so they don't need to pull away.

Apart from that I am making what I call a Rogues Gallery, and Lily has done me a lovely title in heavy gothic script. This is a collection of pen portraits of all the members of the group. I am quite open about it and they can look over my shoulder any time and see what I'm writing and make their own comments. 'My mother says my hair is mouse, not brown – no one has brown hair. What colour is mouse anyway?' I let them make their own suggestions for my pen portraits but as some of these are highly personal and not always very flattering I don't necessarily include them, or perhaps I modify them so that no one will be hurt. For example, 'Seb's hair sticks up like a guineapig's' is quite amusingly expressive and accurate but I doubt Seb would like to see it that way so I change it to 'Seb's hair is not all brushed in the same direction.' Similarly 'Rupert shouldn't shout out like he does' becomes 'Rupert sometimes speaks in a very loud voice.' The boys and girls take a dim view of this pussyfooting censorship and some of them have taken to creating their own Rogues' Galleries though they have kept them pretty close to their chests, albeit dropping heavy and provocative hints about the contents which is a source of trouble, or else use them to taunt people – 'I've said your feet turn in like a penguin's' – which is also a source of trouble! Anna-one has absolutely forbidden me to include a portrait of her in my collection but she can't prevent the others from doing so. She continues in her own corner writing away and covering her work as if people were trying to see it which they aren't. She mutters as she writes like a witch casting spells.

You must be beginning to think I've got an odd lot here and in a way I have. One thing to remember in judging them (and in judging what I am doing with them) is that almost all these children are rejects or failures in some way or other. Only one or two seem to have normal backgrounds, as in having come to Clouds from prep school and with a complete set of parents. Some left or were 'taken away' from another school, and at least four of them have step-parents, some of them with problems of their own. Stella seems to have several sets of sort-of parents and to live in about five different places. Two live abroad and only see their parents twice a year – to them school is more like home than home is. In fact school acts as a kind of refuge, offering a security and stability that they don't otherwise have. Here they can metaphorically – or literally in Freda's case – sit and suck their thumbs!

Principle 10: In many cases school is not so much about <u>making</u> children as <u>repairing</u> them. It's not a factory but a hospital (or a nursing home perhaps).

May 12 A Real Live Ghost

I got a bit of a shock the other evening: I saw a ghost! And what was it a ghost of? Myself! And yet not myself but myself-and-another. And who was that other? Minkie!

This is what happened. Robbie's ghost story that I told you about, while far from frightening in itself, nonetheless puts me the reader and typist of it into a sort of spooky frame of mind. For the sake of the writer I try to get into the appropriate mood and give the story every possible chance of success, even subtly making the odd change as I type (and hope he doesn't notice). I was up quite late on this job – late enough to need a light to read by, i.e. a candle. Having the light inside meant that the windows – no curtains, you remember – go black and become mirrors. Well, something prompted me to get up holding my candle – it's a chamber-stick like Wee Willie Winkie's ! – and go over to the window on the seaward side. What I saw was myself, of course, though looking a bit spooky from the candle throwing shadows up my face. Then suddenly there was another face alongside mine, a disembodied face, half in darkness, half lit through the glass by the light from my candle. Then that face shifted and aligned itself with my reflection in the window-mirror so that there was the impression of my face being overshadowed – no, overtaken, taken over – by this other one. It had become me, I it, to create something new – some<u>one</u> new – a different person. <u>I</u> had not ceased to be but had become someone else or perhaps become in a moment the self I would be in about ten years' time.

Was I scared! The other face was familiar but I couldn't immediately place it, it seemed to come out of the darkness but when a few minutes later there was a knock at the door I nearly jumped out of my skin. Having jumped back into my skin I opened the door to Minkie and realised it was his face I'd seen outside, his face that had combined so eerily with mine.

Of course I was relieved but also shaking though I tried not to show it. I couldn't really say, 'I thought you were a ghost'! He said, 'I saw your light. Care for a swim?' He had a towel round his neck. Well in truth I didn't much care for the idea but I didn't want to seem feeble and unadventurous to a man whose educational philosophy is that one should do as much as possible all the time, 'carpe diem' – though in this case 'carpe noctem' for heavens' sake! Also I thought a splash might calm my nerves after that unnerving experience. So I grabbed my things and down the Dell path we went I would like to say by the light of the moon but actually more by the remaining light of day and the overspill of artificial light from the mainland shore on the other side of the Solent. Minkie had no torch so I didn't bring mine.

The tide was fairly full. The sea was black. I've never swum in the dark before except in a pool and to tell the truth I didn't fancy it at all. How were you to know what was in or under the water? Well of course there was no reason to think it would be any different from in the day when there was never anything to be bothered by – not exactly shark-infested waters, the Solent! But who was to say a great shoal of jellyfish hadn't wobbled their way into the bay? How friendly does 'Portugese man-o'-war' sound to you?!

To my surprise, as I walked gingerly down into the innocent little waves wondering how far I was going to get, Minkie was clambering on to the rocks at the end. Why get in there, I wondered, when to my astonishment he threw up his arms and dived into the water. It wasn't from a great height but supposing there were submerged rocks or some great plank of flotsam floating darkly invisible on the waters? I held my breath as he must have done because he didn't surface until some moments later and then proceeded to swim strongly across the bay to the headland at the other end, some distance away. I swam about a bit well within my depth trying not to imagine things coming into contact with my body but actually quite enjoying the phosphorescence whirling about my arms as I swam (never seen that before). The water seemed less cold than usual though it's not exactly warm at this time of year. Minkie swam to the further headland – at least I suppose he did because he was actually out of sight for a while – and then swam back, as I said, quite a distance but he is a very strong swimmer as I told you.

After that little excursion we returned to my bothy where I made tea on the primus I've installed there and we talked till about 3 a.m. He really is an extraordinary man with an incredibly wide range of knowledge as well as a powerful intellect. We talked a lot about education and I told him about the idea Val and I had for Rawle and he was very interested though in his opinion the on-the-job apprenticeship-type learning we had in mind only really works if it is backed up by more theoretical opportunities, i.e. a school with professional teachers. He is all in favour of practical experience, hence all the visits to places and activities outside as well as inside school viz the mill at Newtown and the farm here. He's one of those people who seems to have read everything and he told me there is a movement in America towards 'destructuring' (I think that was the word) destructuring education. This comes from people who want to destructure everything anyway apparently from governments and the whole world order downwards including the capitalist system, religion, conventional morality, government – the lot. (Sounds more like destructing than destructuring to me!) The only destructuring he could support would be like Mao's action he told me about of closing down the whole educational system in China for an entire year in order to restructure it. "The medium is the message," he said, quoting someone and as if I should know what it meant.

We had a really good chat and he was very supportive of my method (if it can be called that) with Ash which he said was working well in that several of the children had come to life more in other aspects of life at Clouds because of what they were getting from the tutor group, justifying in his opinion the centrality of that element of the school's philosophy. I was very encouraged by this particularly as having asked me about my plans for the future he more or less offered me a permanent position at Clouds. I must say I am very attracted. For one thing here we are in the middle of May, just a few weeks to go to the end of the year and I have nothing lined up for September. Perhaps I should think of doing some training but it's too late to apply now. For another thing I really like it here and feel that the school with Minkie as its Hed is forging something new and highly creative in education, also that I am finding my feet at last. Of course I don't much like being at this much of a distance from Rawle and London, leave alone Retford, but one can't have everything. I could settle here.

That said, I get the impression that Minkie is having a bit of a struggle. I'm detached from staff politics and gossip and all that sort of thing but it's clear not all staff share his vision or have his energy or interest or drive. He's not a bullying headmaster, he leads by example, but he is inclined to upstage the staff by, for example, writing more in the Day Books than the tutors do themselves and getting too close to the detail of the children's lives which they (the staff) think is their role, not his. He is also too intellectual for their tastes being inclined to make speeches and quote everyone from Bertrand Russell to Sophocles to Levi-Strauss. Somehow this all puts pressure on the staff and they get stressed. You should see the exhaustion on their faces towards the end of the day during the meeting we have after Evening Gathering, they can hardly keep their eyes open some of them. Just as well half-term's coming up, four days and nights might restore them to themselves! Minkie himself, as I've said, doesn't sleep but I've noticed the strain growing in him. When his haggard face appeared alongside mine in the window the other night I was shocked by how he looked almost haunted himself. And now that I think of him swimming furiously from one headland of the bay to another which I felt was his custom at night if not at dawn too for all I know – when I visualise him doing that I feel it's as if he's trying to hold something together, to unite two halves of something, and he's doing, or trying to do it, by sheer drive and perseverance and willpower – and on his own. Can a chap go on like that for ever?

Talking of half-term I shan't be going away but staying here. That will not only save me money but I get paid for it as well, because the job is being in charge of the handful of children who haven't anywhere to go for so short a time. Of course they don't have to be taught or anything, they can ditch their bloody Day Books for a long weekend, but I will have to think up some entertainments for them, drive them off to a funfair or something in the school minibus. The main drawback is that I have to be out of the bothy and into school so as to be in the same building as the children while their houseparents are away. This puts me into the clutches of the Three Witches as they are unkindly known, that is the Matron, Mrs Fawkus, and her two helpers, Mops and Mrs Pinne, who live in a coven at the top of the girls' boarding bit. School kitchens will be closed so that puts me and the children at the mercy of their cooking, I'm told. As according to the children they live entirely on nettle tea harvested with a silver sickle by the light of the full moon I may need to lay in tins of beans. Wish I were with you.

May 19 Unrest!

I said in my last that I thought Minkie was having a bit of a struggle with selling his philosophy to all the staff, particularly some of the longer-serving teachers who were here in Mr Kendall's day – and before that – when obviously things weren't so intense, they didn't have a highly intellectual Hed philosophising at them and resurrecting the school's original vision and they didn't have to work so hard. Now just being here a term I haven't bothered with common room politics and grumbles. (I'm sorry to say that we teachers are rather a grumbly lot who tend to feel put upon and hard done by and unappreciated as well as underpaid of course. And we don't like being told what to do – spend our lives telling other people what to do but reverse the flow ? – no, sir!) Anyway there's a bit of an issue come up and even I can't help being drawn into it. In fact I've been drawn into it.

Yesterday evening as I was sauntering back home (as I call it) after Evening Gathering and the staff meeting the Hedgehog comes up alongside and walks with me. Softens me up by chatting about me and then quizzes me about the training session that Minkie has organised for the staff. Teachers don't like the idea that they might need training at all (they did that at the outset) but what has put the cat among the pigeons and stirred up a hornets' nest (yes, it's as bad as that!) is that he has arranged this training session for the first afternoon of half-term. The children go home at lunchtime on Saturday and normally the staff clear off then too but this time they're to stay till teatime so that this training, which is a visiting speaker on child psychology or something, can take place. Well, clearly the Hedgehog is going around rattling his prickles (no, that's a porcupine, isn't it!) stirring up discontent about this. How do I feel about it, he enquires. Losing a precious half day of a holiday that's too short anyway, just like everyone else I've been working hard, doing great stuff with Ash (flatter, flatter) don't I feel a bit miffed about being required to stick around for this extra work? Well, as it happens I've got to stick around anyway so it doesn't bother me that the first hour or two of the half-term 'holiday' is taken up listening to someone on education. I don't want to sound too pi though so I don't come out strongly but then as we reach my bothy he produces a sheet of paper and says, 'A lot of people have signed this. It's a protest we plan to deliver to M.A. Perhaps you'd care to add your signature.' He's pressing now. Well, I can but look. 'We, the undersigned members of the teaching staff feel it is unreasonable that we should be required to… extremely hard-working six and a half days a week… not the time to expect people to… etc.' I hesitate. Not to sign is to undermine my colleagues' position; there is such a thing as staff solidarity. But the truth is I don't actually share their view so why should I sign? Luckily the Hedgehog sees me demurring and backs off. 'I can see… being new and only temporary… no, I understand.' He pockets up his precious sheet and waddles back up the path no doubt looking for any other slugs and snails he might lure into his lunch-box!

May 22 Half-Term

Well here I am, in the Sick Room. No, not sick but just my quarters as I explained in my last letter, for half-term. The Three Witches haven't got homes of their own to go to, I gather, so they're staying over like me. God knows what they have by way of bedrooms but they share a sitting room which has a sofa, chairs and a telly and they have kindly invited me to share it with them when I'm free. I don't like to do this, partly because I feel a bit awkward and out-of-place, partly because you get kippered in there as all three of them smoke <u>all</u> the time, plus the telly is on <u>all</u> the time even when there's no one watching it. Mrs Fawkus is the presiding deity, being Matron, whereas the other two, whatever their titles, are clearly lesser beings. There's Mops, as she's called, (surely not her real name) who says very little and that in a Welsh accent which is very charming though her face is like slate. Then there's Mrs Pinne who's a dwarf. I don't mean very small but actually a dwarf with that rolling gait they have. She's incredibly cheerful and always cracking jokes. Considering she spends her day counting handkerchiefs and darning socks her cheerfulness seems pretty miraculous. It doesn't look like a great life to me, certainly not in accord with the 'carpe diem' philosophy of Clouds where the world is a place of opportunity, wonder and discovery, but I gather they've all been here forever and they seem to be perfectly content in spite of their jobs and their living conditions, and I expect they're paid a pittance. It's in the companionship I suppose – instead of seizing the day they're quietly ambling through it together. 'Fellowship' indeed. Rather enviable really.

Oh but I didn't tell you about the training session drama. I heard that the Hedgehog's letter of petition-cum-protest that I didn't sign was presented to Minkie but he didn't bow to it and the 'beginning-of-half-term detention' as the staff called it went ahead. Or rather it wasn't cancelled officially but Minkie was tipped off by Mr Murphy (the second master) that there was to be a mass no-show. And what did I do? Well, I wasn't going to join the boycotters as Minkie had only just as good as offered me a job after all, so I lingered in the ante-hall showing willing in case something went ahead. I couldn't bear to think of Minkie turning up with his guest to find no audience at all. About ten minutes after the starting time I was still standing around in that atmosphere of almost eerie silence that falls upon a school when the children have left it, and then I slunk away.

I don't know quite what will happen about this. It is surely most unusual for an entire common room to disobey, to defy, their head in this way. What will Minkie do? I suppose in an ordinary school with an ordinary head it would be a case for the governors who would either have to give the head their support or support the staff but there's nothing ordinary about Minkie and as I've mentioned he's here on the basis of being virtually autonomous. He's not around now so I guess he's gone away to think about it. I feel rather sorry for him. It's not his fault he's a dynamo who makes the rest of us feel like duds and he's certainly doing his best for the school. He's not married and doesn't seem to have any private life or relationships so he's in effect on his own surrounded by enemies. Perhaps that's why he spends quite a lot of time here with me and why I'm happy to talk to him. I feel quite flattered as not many people in my situation (i.e. just starting out and being a very junior member of staff) get the chance of any length of time with their head and I think I'm learning a lot.

The children temporarily in my charge are a mixed bunch, none from my Tutor Group, and though they're obviously glad not to be working they're thoroughly bored and keep asking me if we can go out here, there and everywhere which I do my best to indulge as I feel sorry for them being stuck here when everyone else is enjoying the freedom of home. There's a girl in the Sixth Form called Tamsin Lightwater who's seventeen-going-on-twenty-one who's particularly restive but there's nothing I can do to provide for her needs.

Surprise encounter yesterday. I'd taken the children along to Helensbridge for some sailing where the school has boats. Not being much of a sailor myself I was a bit concerned about letting them out on their own or with each other but it was an unwindy sort of day and they were lifejacketed up to the gills and seemed to know what they were doing so I let them get on with it (all except Tamsin who remained in the minibus glowering) and sat myself down on a bench in the sunshine. Hadn't been there long when I was hailed by a familiar voice – 'Clarke!' It was Mr (or as I still think of him, Major) Oakes of Eaton House calling to me from a parked car nearby. He was in the driver's seat and next to him was an old lady whom he introduced through the window as his mother. I knew he had an old mum but hadn't really hauled that fact in let alone met her. She didn't seem up to much.

He's not a great small talker, Mr Oakes, but we exchanged a few bits about Eaton House and Clouds, then he surprised me by saying, 'Been meaning to write to you. Something I wanted to talk to you about,' and invited me to have lunch with him at the hotel in Solentside (not far away) where he and his mother were staying. 'They do quite a decent bit of plaice there,' he said. As I explained about my responsibilities he swept the bay with a sceptical eye as if to prove to himself that I was inventing these children but under pressure from him I agreed to set them up at the fish and chip shop and give them a couple of hours unsupervised while I ate my plaice with him and his mother in politer surroundings – I could do with a good meal. But I can't think what he should want to talk to me about.

May 25 An Offer on a Plate

I duly turned up at the hotel in Solentside. I'd dressed up

a bit for the occasion knowing what a stickler for formality the major is. Just as well I did as there he was in white shirt and cravat and blazer with the regimental buttons. He even had white shoes on – you'd think it was 1932! Just as well also because the hotel was a very stuffy old-fashioned place.

There they both were, old Mrs Oakes and the major, already ensconced at their table in the dining room, the old lady in her wheelchair pulled up to her place. It was a lovely summer's day but the room was stuffy and the shining sea on the other side of the huge plateglass window was so fresh and attractive I felt almost claustrophobic. All the other customers looked rich and old. Still it was quite nice to have waiters and waitresses fussing about – I even had my napkin spread across my lap for me. It made me feel like a small boy but also very grand at the same time – Little Lord Fauntleroy! Then it was a glass of sherry – zing! I haven't had a drink for weeks.

Then came soup. Mrs Oakes had trouble with that because her hands shake so much and only about half of what she started with actually made it to her mouth and even then quite a lot of it dribbled down her chin. This might have been embarrassing but Major Oakes took it in his stride and she wasn't in the least concerned about it herself. It was almost as if she were an infant as her son dabbed her chin for her with his napkin. She didn't say anything at all so for conversational purposes she could be ignored. She made quite an odd picture, come to think of it, because although very old and obviously infirm she looked at the same time very healthy. Her hair which is still quite thick (though an odd and unnatural colour) was very neatly coiffeured and she had a smooth plump face that was very far from the haggard wrinkles you associate with old age.

The famous fish arrived underneath huge silver domes big enough to hide a boar's head. These covers were then lifted up with an expert flourish by three waiters simultaneously, Mrs Oakes' fish was deftly filleted by the head waiter and we all set to. Major Oakes didn't seem in any hurry to get down to talking about whatever it was he'd invited me for, as if the meal itself were some sort of sacred rite that shouldn't be disrespected by anything as common as a purposeful conversation. So it wasn't until the syllabub had been cleared away and coffee had been ordered that he actually got round to the purpose of the occasion. 'There's room for a young man at Eaton House,' he said, just like that, in a rather blunt and direct way but looking out of the window at the same time. Well, that was clear enough! Oh dear, I thought, if only he knew how far I've come since Christmas, how deeply involved I am at Clouds and what a very different place it is from his curious establishment. 'It's doing rather well,' he said. 'Room for improvement though.' Then he asked me if I'd got any ideas – for improvement, that is, which was surprising because he's never asked me for my opinion on anything before. I suggested bigger premises, it was all a bit cramped. 'Expense,' he muttered. 'Still might be right. Job for a younger man anyway.' Another clear hint.

The dining room was emptying by this time and the old lady had fallen asleep. Then he said, 'Expect I'll be retiring soon. Old lady's pretty much a full-time job. Seems a pity to let the place go. Long might take it on but…' They unswaddled Mrs Oakes of her napkins and he wheeled her out, saying goodbye to me in the foyer and nothing more about Eaton House or my possible future there.

Well, what do you think of that?!

Now I must go and see what's become of my charges – they want to go bowling tonight – hey ho! Still, it's the last night of half-term and my boarding duties are coming to an end.

Johnny.

May 30

Many thanks, Fi, for your thoughts about Eaton House and Major Oakes' offer. As you can imagine I've been having a pretty good think about it too, because in effect he's offering me the headship – not immediately of course but in a year or two. Imagine – me! – a headmaster at twenty-four. Quite something, eh? Of course you're right that the place is not exactly in the forefront of educational thought (to put it mildly) and you're right that academically it's rather below me. Wouldn't I miss teaching the older pupils, doing literary criticism and so on? Well, you've got a point. It seems a bit of a waste of a respectable Oxford degree to coach boys for a low-level and antiquated exam like Common Entrance, I agree. But maybe Eaton House isn't such a dead end. Maybe there's a huge opportunity here and I've been working something up in my imagination – you know, rather as you and Onjon did at Rawle. You're right of course that I would need to find out more about the financial side of things, whether there are any borrowings and what the accounts look like. I don't want to put all my eggs into a sinking ship (as it were!). But look at it this way: Major Oakes spoke of expansion. Well now suppose that were financially possible, suppose he was willing to invest some of his profits into acquiring new premises, getting out of that dreary St Botolphs place to somewhere bigger and better – a whole house perhaps – with a lawn for the boys to kick a ball about on instead of circling half a ping-pong table like prisoners on exercise. As I strolled along the beach in the unending light of a midsummer's evening this vision came to me. It was a vision of sunlight streaming into a spacious classroom, pictures on the walls, happy children working eagerly away under the eye of enthusiastic staff supported by all modern amenities.

'The Proprietor and Headmaster of Eaton House Preparatory School, Hampstead, announce the relocation of the establishment to number 49 Lindfield Road. This substantial property has been purpose-renovated and fitted out with the latest educational facilities including science and language laboratories. The school will continue to offer the supreme advantage of small classes that countless academic studies have shown to be crucial to success and in which each boy will work at the level best suited to his particular aptitudes and with a maximum of individual attention from the school's team of highly qualified and experienced tutors.'

Technology – that's the cry of the new era, isn't it? Modern parents will respond to that idea. 'A language lab, eh? – that's the thing – all I had was a scruffy old text book.' And there'll be a TV in every room. Let's face it, for good or ill, this is a telly generation, not a book generation, it's brought up on 'the box' from babyhood, so why not teach it through the medium of the age? That will maximise their learning and transform their entire educational experience. 'No more Latin, no more French, no more sitting on the old school bench.' Well, there would still be Latin and French, of course, but it would be taught in such a way that the children would positively enjoy the experience and therefore *learn*. Soon the television would be doing half their teaching for them.

And there's this 'dyslexia' business that Val was on to. A lot of those Eaton House boys, now that I came to think about it, had that problem. They had been written off as dunces because they couldn't spell but actually a lot of them were quite intelligent if you looked past the awful spelling and being hopeless at French – they just needed special treatment for that special need. And the new Eaton House would provide that. Then it would soon get a reputation for taking boys that the mainstream had discarded as incapable and putting them firmly back on to the high road of conventional academic performance. Admittedly the school might at first be thought of as taking 'the failures' but that would soon change as the parents saw the improvement – they would be glowing with pleasure and gratitude as their sulky and awkward dimbos are transformed into bright-eyed achievers. Then it wouldn't be long before I'd have a mother gushing, 'Oh, Mr Clarke, you've done such a *wonderful* job with Andrew – we're *thrilled* he's got into Mill Hill – we'd just *so* love it if you could take Daniel. Trouble is he's only ten but he's *dying* to come here. Is there *any* chance you could open up a junior class?'

And then pretty soon we'd be buying the house next door and connecting the two with an extension containing dining room and library to become a full-scale prep school – not of course on the dreadful old lines of Latin and detention and caning but on a fresh prospectus of learning with enjoyment, with stimulation by the fruits of modern educational thinking and research, reinforced by technical aids undreamt of in an earlier benighted age. How's that for 'progressive'? How's that for 'in the forefront of educational thinking'?!

Well, that's my vision. Not so unrealistic is it? I'm really excited about it – much more than about sitting around talking about *Hamlet* with teenagers, to be honest. And Major Oakes is handing me this opportunity on a plate. Could anyone expect anything better? Now it's just a matter of putting pen to paper and composing a 'prospectus'. If Major Oakes is serious about this I know he'll buy my idea – in fact he'll be bowled over.

The only problem is here. In the last of the day's light I can just see Minkie making his way over to his diving rock for his nightly swim. Now how am I going to tell him I won't be staying on at Clouds after all?

Meanwhile it's business as usual here. The 'atmosphere' isn't getting any sweeter and I don't believe Minkie can get any thinner without disappearing altogether! Oh well, not long to the end of term and a well-earned rest for all the staff; things'll settle down after that, I expect. I feel as if I've known my group half a lifetime, we have become quite used to each other – I could say fond of each other. I could never have imagined such a thing two months ago.

Johnny.

June 9

Thanks very much for your letter, Fi, and the leaflet. It presents Rawle very attractively, I think, and the line drawings with the map and everything are very effective – for example the clock in the stable yard on one side with the clock on the church tower on the other, and the view over the lake to Hangar Wood. Then the list of things to see and do – well, it's a day's work, isn't it?! I hadn't realised the home farm had come on so strongly with the milking demonstrations and the rare breeds not to mention the two great shire horses with their show prizes and brasses alongside the ploughing machinery and wagons.

I suppose your idea is to spread it round the locality, to hotels and places, to bring people in, and I expect you've sent a copy to the local paper. It's not going to have the big game appeal of Woburn but the clever part of it is that it appeals to old and young, with the old being able to say things like 'I remember using a hay-rake like that on my grandfather's farm before the war,' while the children can have pony rides and handle the ducklings. Seems a long time since I was at Rawle. I shall be free from here in a month. Perhaps I could get to you for the fête which I see from your timetable of events is July 20. If I come and stay a day or two before that I could help with setting it up. Would that be OK? Incidentally I'm wondering what you thought about my vision for Eaton House that I wrote about in my last letter.

My Ash are much less Trash by the day though I can't say it's all plain sailing now that the first sort of honeymoon period is over after our move here to the bothy. Robbie, for example, continues in more or less constant trouble, the only time he isn't is when he's with me so I try and keep him in here as much as possible even when I have to be somewhere else. It's a bit like keeping crime down by keeping thieves in jail – at least if they're locked up they can't go around robbing people! He is now on his third ghost story. This one is called 'The Witches of Monkstone' and draws heavily on Mrs Fawkus, Mops and Mrs Pinne who have been cruelly converted from an innocent trio of telly-watching, tea-drinkers into a coven of malicious spell-casters! I have a feeling there's going to be a violent confrontation between them and the monk, the hero of Volume 1, 'The Monk of Monkstone,' though it's equally possible that there will be a surprise visit from outer space. The surprise will probably be as much of one to the author as to the reader as he writes at breakneck speed without much, if any, idea of what will happen next or why. He considers himself inspired! Oh well, it keeps him out of mischief and at least he's got something to show for his efforts whatever its merit or lack of it. Another good development is that he is learning to type (on my machine) for himself so that is saving me a lot of time. Minkie is keeping up with the story too and giving encouragement.

The man himself, incidentally, seems ever more thin and gaunt. There were no 'consequences' of the staff strike over the half-term training session but the general atmosphere is hardly a happy and peaceful one. No one (I mean on the staff) seems to speak to him if they can help it. As you know I just get on with my own job.

Back to the children. The half-term break has not been good for Stella. After her Barbados (or Zermatt) jaunt at Easter it took some time to get her to calm down and give her attention to something beside ' having a good time with boys'. Of course there are still boys here and she is working her way through the Sixth Form but before half-term she was actually doing some work but then a long weekend in London has derailed her again and she seems in a state of frivolous excitement interspersed with periods of sullen withdrawal. Anna-one isn't becoming any more human and Tom has now switched from football to beach-ball which is an American game, I think, that involves punching a ball over a high net in the sand. They love it and the weather is helping.

You were wondering whether one or two of the children might be becoming too dependent on me, perhaps too attached to me, or indeed me to them! 'Don't let them take over your life!' you say. Well, you're right, that is a risk, they are just adolescents in the first place and then several of them, as I've said, are emotionally hungry and in need of something or someone to attach themselves to (though to some extent aren't we all?!) I suppose because to me they are 'my children' I'm not realising that I might be more to one or two of them than a temporary substitute parent. In fact the other day I found a little piece of paper under my pillow that had the conventional heart with an arrow through it with 'JC' at the pointed end and a '?!' at the feathery end. I am always a bit surprised when it appears that someone fancies me. I say 'always' as if it were happening all the time! – when what I mean is 'whenever it does, occasionally, happen'! I'm not sure what I can do about that. As I will probably not be here next term and there's barely a month to go to the end of this term I guess it's nothing much to worry about. As for their importance to me I think it would be 'another year, another lot' if I were here again in September. (I look forward to hearing what you thought about my vision for Eaton House. I have sent my 'prospectus' to Major Oakes and expect to hear back from him any day. I'll let you know the response.)

Thanks again – Johnny.

June 15

Dear Fi,

News from Eaton House at last! Not good news – though not about my plans. I've had a letter from the school secretary telling me that one of the members of staff has died – well, killed himself actually. There was a nice chap called Paget who was not a great teacher but he was a lovely man who did all the handyman jobs around the place and was probably happier at that sort of thing than the job he was paid for, which was teaching maths. He didn't seem an unhappy sort of person at all and certainly his wife was very cheerful – in fact they seemed a happy middle-aged couple who were quite content to live their neat and ordinary lives in a very unmodern way. I went to lunch there once. The sitting room was full of pictures and mementoes of the war – he was a mechanic on aircraft. I don't know what can have possessed him to shut himself up in his Dormobile (which he had fitted out as a mini workshop) and turn on the gas. Nobody knows why he did it. The school secretary, Fay Palfreyman, writes, 'it is not only a great tragedy but a mystery as well.' As it happens she was very fond of him and at this lunch she told me he had had to deal with some pretty gruesome stuff in those planes coming back from raids over Germany. Perhaps they were nagging at his imagination, some images from that experience, though you'd think such things would fade with time. She writes, 'it has been a terrible shock to everyone'. I can imagine how upset and confused the boys at Eaton House will be. Probably most of them won't ever have been that close to a dead person as to him: one day teaching them algebra, the next gone – how can they make sense of that? And he was such a nice man too, everyone liked him even if the boys took advantage of him. The more I think about it the sadder I feel…

I'll write again soon.

Love, Johnny.

21 June Clouds

Dear Fi,

Astonishing news here. Minkie, the Hed, has disappeared! He hasn't gone up in a puff of smoke (as far as we know!), but he simply isn't here any more and nobody knows where he's gone. Obviously heads slip away from time to time just to get a breather but they always tell their deputy and leave him in charge till they get back. Well, Murphy (the deputy) doesn't know anything about it. We all turned up for Morning Gathering as usual but no Minkie. Murphy slips out to try and find him while we wait. He comes back a few minutes later looking a bit rattled and breathless but acting calm. 'The Hed is not available this morning,' he says and carries out a shortened form of the meeting before we all go off to Tutor Group. Nothing to worry about there and probably only the staff thought anything of it. Word gets round quietly that all staff must be in the common room for morning break and there Murphy tells us that the truth is he is unable to find the Hed anywhere – he isn't in the office or in his flat and he (Murphy) knows that the Hed would not just not turn up – if he was unable or indisposed in some way he would let him know. There was probably no need to worry, he said, 'but the official line must be that he's not well and that should head off any other questions. If he's not back or we've got no other news I shall get in touch with the Convener' (that's the name for the chairman of Conclave) 'and he must take the matter from there.' Now it's well known that Murphy doesn't like Minkie but he is loyal to the school and has some self-respect so he doesn't do or say anything (publicly at any rate) to undermine his headmaster but there was a curious mixture in his manner of anxiety and relish – partly 'This is something big and I'm in charge', and partly 'I knew he was an unstable man and now I'm proved right', with a hint of 'This could be the start of better things.' I don't much like Murphy. However, when he said was there anything anyone had to say that might possibly give any clues I thought I'd better tell him about the towel.

June 25 Clouds

Dear Fi,

The search goes on! More of that soon. I just thought I'd let you know I've had a letter from Major Oakes – short and unsweet as I would expect from him, particularly in view of the tragedy they've experienced at Eaton House. He describes my prospectus as 'a grand plan' but says he's 'going to have to pour cold water on it'. He says the St Botolphs PCC have decided to increase the rent on the school premises and on top of that 'the numbers for this coming September are not very good.' He blames the public schools 'who will now take virtually any boy whatever they get in C.E.' 'The long and the short of this is,' he goes on, 'I've decided to draw stumps at the end of next summer.' Then (mixing his metaphors somewhat) he describes the waters as 'fished out' and so 'that's the end of it.' His letter ends with 'Sorry about this. Hope it's not too disappointing. Best wishes for your career. I'm sure you'll do well. Yours truly.'

So much for that then. If I wasn't caught up in the drama here I'd have time to register some feelings about this. Am I disappointed? I don't know. You never gave me yr opinion of my 'prospectus' but you did raise a few questions at the outset that suggest you maybe thought it wasn't the ideal thing for me anyway so perhaps you're thinking I'm well out of it. You may be right. On the other hand everything's up in the air here and anyone thinking ahead must be wondering what the future is for Clouds. The police have been round so there's no keeping it from the children and everyone's sure that it will be in the press soon – <u>and then what</u>?!

June 29 Clouds

Dear Fi,

Thank you so much for what my mother would call

'sympathetic noises' regarding developments in my life – extraordinary that two such dreadful things should happen at virtually the same time. Well, I say 'dreadful' but we still don't know what's become of Minkie – whether he has suffered a 'dreadful' fate that we are yet to learn of, or what. But whatever the case with him it is certainly 'dreadful' as far as the school is concerned. We (i.e. the staff) are all working flat out to try and keep things normal and give the children some sense of stability even though we can't actually give them any real reassurance.

I mentioned the police coming here. Well one of the officers had his turn with me and I thought I couldn't do better than write up the conversation from memory even though of course it can't be accurate word for word.

Please tell us what you can, Mr Clarke. You never know what details might be helpful. You were closer to Mr Arkwright than many of the staff, I understand.

Perhaps I was, I saw quite a lot of him recently. Several evenings a week he'd call in here before, sometimes after, his swim and we'd chat.

What about?

The school, the children, education. I think he felt I truly shared his vision so he was quite relaxed talking to me.

Which he wasn't with other members of staff. There was quite a lot of resistance to his ideas and his leadership, wasn't there?

Yes, there was – there is.

Would you say he was hated?

I wouldn't put it as strongly as that.

But some staff wanted to get rid of him, didn't they?

Yes, I think so but – heavens! – not in the sense of …

Of killing him?

Good Lord, no! I don't imagine for a moment that anyone here would dream of –

Murders take place among ordinary people, Mr Clarke.

Is this a murder enquiry, Inspector?

At the moment it's a missing person inquiry. Now tell me about the towel please.

The towel. Well, that morning I went down to the beach quite early as I often do if it's fine.

And Mr Arkwright wasn't there.

He's usually earlier than me.

And there you saw the towel.

Yes.

And what did you think?

I thought – I assumed he'd left it behind after his swim.

So you…

So I picked it up and brought it back to school. That's when we realised something was up when he didn't appear at Morning Gathering and his deputy didn't know anything about it.

When you picked up the towel from the rocks was there anything else there?

Not that I noticed.

How did you know it was his. It had no name on. Did you recognise it?

(I was beginning to realise what is meant by 'Being questioned by the police.' Was I a suspect?!)

Not exactly. I just assumed it was his because it was in his usual place, the place he always dives off from.

Do you dive from there?

I don't much like diving.

You're aware that, depending on the tide, it can be deep and there are hidden rocks?

Yes. But Mr Arkwright knew the place well, and he was an Olympic swimmer, you know.

So I'm told. What is the evidence for that?

Well, everyone knows it.

How do they know it?

I suppose he's told people.

Would you consider that good evidence?

Not in itself but I've seen him swimming and I can categorically say he's a strong swimmer.

Strong enough to swim out into the shipping lane, for example, or to the Martello tower opposite the bay?

I should say so. Why, is that important?

If he could swim that far out he could get picked up. He

would have no possible identification on him and he wouldn't have to tell his rescuers who he was. Mind if I look around your room, Mr Clarke?

Of course not – go ahead.

(That felt a bit odd, I can tell you. He wasn't exactly rummaging in drawers or anything but I thought, 'Well what on earth is he actually looking for?' Anyway nothing came of this 'search'.)

Did Mr Arkwright ever talk to you about the future of the school? His plans for it?

Our talk was more about educational ideals and practices than plans.

Did he indicate in any way that he would like you to be part of the school's future?

Well, he was complimentary about my work.

Did he offer you a job – a continued position at the school?

Not exactly offer me a job.

But he made it clear that he favoured you and that he wanted you to stay on at Clouds?

I don't know about 'favoured' exactly but yes, he made it clear he, as I say, approved of what I was doing for the children and would be pleased if I stayed on.

And did you encourage him to think that you would?

Well I did until recently when I started having other ideas.

Did you tell him about those other ideas?

No.

You just went cool on the prospect of staying at Clouds?

I suppose you could put it like that.

Mr Arkwright was – is – unmarried. He doesn't seem to have had any close relationships – no girlfriend, for example.

I've no idea.

You didn't talk about such things?

No. His private life was a completely closed book. I think the school was his whole life actually.

Did he ever ask you about your private life, Mr Clarke?

No.

May I ask, do you have a girlfriend?

Not at the moment, no.

Did Mr Arkwright ever make any…approaches to you of a personal kind?

'Personal'?

Physical.

Do you mean 'sexual'?

Yes, sexual.

No, he did not – absolutely not.

(I was pretty taken aback by that suggestion as you may imagine. I wonder if some member of staff had been making insinuations.)

I hope you don't mind my asking. We're trying to put together a picture of a man that nobody seems to know much about. Tell me, if you were Mr Arkwright and you were thinking of disappearing, how might you do it?

I've no idea. Does this happen often?

Sometimes people want to escape from their present existence and start again elsewhere – as someone else perhaps.

A sort of temporary suicide.

Exactly.

But why should Mr Arkwright want to do that?

Perhaps things were getting on top of him.

He certainly was under a lot of stress, I agree, but that hardly seems enough to make a man of his talents do something absolutely drastic – like this.

Did he ever talk about his past – his life in New Zealand before he came to England?

Come to think of it, no.

Didn't that seem at all odd?

We were so busy talking about the school and suchlike.

So there was nothing at all to suggest that he might be bothered about anything – beyond school concerns, that is?

No.

That he might have something to hide, say? That there might be something … catching up with him?

No, not at all.

So it would surprise you if Mr Arkwright had committed suicide?

It would surprise me very much. He was so energetic, so full of purpose – he wouldn't, surely.

Unless there was something greater than his energy and his purpose – some negative force stronger than both.

But no body has been found.

True, neither in the water nor on land. And it's unusual for bodies to disappear in the Solent, it's a narrow expanse and not very deep. There are currents of course but we usually catch up with the corpse before long. We've searched the woods and the cliffs. It's not all that easy to hide a body.

No, I don't suppose it is. Perhaps he faked his death, Inspector, planted the towel to make it look as if he'd drowned, give himself time while the search was on to get away.

And start a new life. Quite so. Or someone else planted the towel to make it look like that.

A murderer, do you mean?

Or a kidnapper.

Why on earth would anyone want to kidnap him?

I've no idea, Mr Clarke.

Reading that over, I realise it sounds like something out of a detective novel but I promise I'm not making it up even if it's not word-perfect. It's clear they haven't a clue, the police – I mean literally not a clue, with the exception of the towel he left on the rocks, but that could be interpreted in any or no way at all. For my own part, I don't believe he's dead. If it was from natural causes his body would have been found by now; if he killed himself like Mr Paget why go to obscure trouble to make a disappearing act of it? Once you're dead, after all, you have no control over what becomes of you, and if the sea hasn't got you (as appears to be the case) where can you be? So I believe he's still alive and I am distressed to think of the distress he must have felt to go and do what he's done.

Thanks again for writing. It's a comfort to hear from you – and a comfort to write to you.

With love from Johnny.

July 6 Clouds

Dear Fi,

The end of the summer term should be a great time but I can hardly tell you how ghastly things are here. I don't know how we're going to get through another week – and even that is with ending early on account of what's happened, because the authorities just don't think they can keep things going properly any longer than that.

Challenges (as they are called, being the Clouds version of exams, consisting of 'projects' the children do on their own) are now more or less over. In light of what has happened about Minkie they have at least cancelled the so-called Wayfaring which is when the children are taken out to various parts of the Island with rucksacks, given a bob each and told to make their way back to school. I suppose they don't want any children disappearing in addition to the headmaster!

As to that, now that it's in the national press, you probably know as much about it as I do, though of course there isn't anything to know. Here of course speculation is rife. Some people reckon his disappearance is to do with money, shady dealings in the past. Why is so little known about his life before he came here? Some people think it's shadier than that and to do with his personal life, and the fantasy mill is grinding overtime on that one! Has he disappeared on purpose in order to pop up somewhere else in the world under a new name? Then there are those who think he has done away with himself, either by drowning, swimming out into the Solent until drowning by sheer exhaustion or by deliberately putting himself in the path of some great ship in the dark. That might explain why no body has been found as he would have been all minced up. Ugh! Nobody believes in the murder or kidnapping idea.

The Convenor and other members of the Conclave have appeared and talked to us to try to keep things calm and we have constant staff meetings to try and hold things together under Murphy's direction. There's an element of guiltiness in this as the staff realise that if Minkie killed himself it might have been owing to stress or depression made worse if not actually brought on by staff objecting to his way of running the school and for example actually going on strike over the half-term training issue. There is no speculation about the school's future at these meetings, just a concentration on seeing things through as normally as possible to the end of term. It's the Dunkirk spirit!

It's actually my tutor group I'm most concerned about. Two – Stella and Freda – have left already. Stella probably bullied her indulgent parents into giving her an early start to her well-earned (I don't think) holidays, and Freda because her over-sensitive parents are worried about the emotional effect on her of being here in the present climate. And they're not the only ones, which is very worrying as regards the future of the school because who knows whether they will actually come back. There's another worrying question: who would choose Clouds as the school for their child with this hanging over it? Will the school still be in business in September? A serious question for all of us, including one who was reckoning to be staying on. What am I going to do now?!

But back to the children. Of course they too speculate endlessly about Minkie and come up with ever more weird and wonderful ideas than even the newspapers, e.g. he's been captured by aliens and taken away in a spaceship, or even that he is an alien himself, disguised (but not very well in their opinion) as a human being who had come down to earth to implant alien neurons into the brains of the Clouds children who would then become superhuman and conquer the world. Anna-one is convinced she's seen him in the woods on the cliffs but nobody believes that any more than they believe the alien fantasy. Robbie predictably is into his next volume entitled 'Minkie and the Monk', Minkie having died and become a ghost and joined forces with his pre-existing 'hero' to terrorise the innocent children of Clouds. I suspect there's going to be a power struggle between them and the three witches, the Fawki as he has termed them, and who knows who will eventually triumph in that conflict? King Kong, I shouldn't wonder!

I make light of all this because the truth is I don't feel all that secure myself. I no longer feel good about being here on my own at night with my candle or in the dark, lying in bed in the silence with the stars twinkling beyond the roof-lights above me. And I don't look out of the windows in the dark.

Should I let the children go on with their fantasies? I can hardly stop them and maybe it's their way of coping with an impossible situation. Now that some children have gone and the normal programme – if it can ever be called that! – has virtually broken down my tutor group seems to have expanded with the addition of several waifs and strays from other groups whose tutors are no doubt glad to see the back of them, so that the bothy has turned into a sort of day-long club-room where people sit about and chat and draw and knit (yes, that's the latest thing, believe it or not!), and drink my coffee.

Though I say it myself, I think the place offers some kind of security, it's a communal retreat, and though they don't say as much the fact that I'm there is obviously important. For example more than once I've had 'You will be here next term, won't you, Mr C.?' This is hard to answer when the truth is it can't be confidently said that anyone will be here next term. I try to be as unschoolmasterly as I can, I think that's what they need. We staff are, after all, 'in loco parentis'. There is a play by a man called Arthur Miller called 'All My Sons' in which the main character – well, I won't try and summarise the story but it's about a man whose job in the war is making bomber aeroplanes – and he comes in the end to realise that it is not only his own son, who is killed in one of these planes to his great grief obviously, but all the young men who meet the same fate are in a sense his sons. 'They were all my sons,' he concludes (in so many words). Well, it might sound a bit emotional and exaggerated but that's how I feel particularly at the moment as I'm sure you can understand. Of course I – and they – have to remember that though I'm now 'in place of a parent' this is not a permanent arrangement.

Funnily enough one of the only positive and useful people around is Tom. His beach volleyball has become a sort of obsession, a craze. At first – I mean straight after Minkie's disappearance – the bay was kind of unofficially out-of-bounds. The image of the towel left on the rocks made everyone feel the place was not just sort of haunted but that if they went down there to walk or swim they might come across Minkie's body. I walk there, wondering about him, trying to think if there was anything in our talks that might give a clue to his fate – or his whereabouts. But I see nothing – or rather what I see is the image of him as he appeared through the window of the bothy that evening when I held the candle up and saw him through the glass as if he was becoming a part of me or I was melting into being him. But I try not to dwell on that. So I picture him diving from his rock and swimming across to the other headland as if he was trying to tie two things together. While everyone (including me) is feeling unsettled Tom – who is as sensitive as a concrete block – just carries on with his game and now almost everyone is in on it, shouting and hurling themselves about on the sand in a physical and competitive frenzy. This is a far better tonic in the circumstances than anything we staff can think up. Good old Tom!

I'm so looking forward to an end to this – and even more I'm looking forward to being at Rawle and seeing everything and everyone again. I'm glad to hear the apple crop is looking promising and as I said perhaps I can be useful over the fête. Thanks for inviting me. You wonder what my plans are for the holidays. Well of course I shall be spending some time with the folks up at Retford (though God knows what I'll actually do there) but of course more pressing is the need to get myself sorted out for September, now that not only Eaton House but Clouds too, in all probability, are non-runners. It's not going to be easy getting something during the summer holidays. Anyway, see you soon.

With love – Johnny.

7

RAWLE

The annual summer fête at Rawle ran pretty much along the lines of the conventional village fête throughout the country. Like any such event it required a massive amount of work on the part of a large number of people, the effort that went into it being quite disproportionate to the monetary proceeds. Lord Nidd – to whom the event was privately known as 'the fête worse than death' – could be heard, though not by his wife, to say, 'It works out at about a bob a man hour, I reckon.' Among those who laboured in the cause there was huge scope for dissension and disparagement, empire building and dereliction of duty, the whole operation masterminded by Lady Nidd with glum resignation, unblessed as she was by nature and in spite of her position with any powers of organisation. Her method, if such it could be called, was to work very hard herself, to delegate none of the responsibilities that had accrued to her over the years, to eschew the use of flattery or cajolery in her armoury of motivation, trusting to each participant's sense of commitment to get the job done. She anticipated no problems, stuck firmly to former practice, intervened in no differences, encouraged no one, corrected no one, chivvied no one, appealed to no one, stomping about in wellingtons – why was the weather preceding the event invariably vile? – prognosticating disaster, magnifying obstacles and harbouring resentments that threatened to boil over into hurtful words. It was the nearest she ever came to being a difficult person.

With the estate's recent development into a commercial business there was a growing feeling that instead of annually mounting this appalling circus there should simply be the allocation of an agreed sum to the maintenance of the church. Rawle had already, with its pony rides, produce stall etc. taken on some of the character of a fête so why duplicate it with such additional effort? This feeling was not given expression, however, for two reasons. The first was that the fête was Lady Nidd's historical domain, allocated to her by custom on marriage and maintained loyally by her ever since, the fact that it was a trial and a tribulation to her being perversely all the more reason in her conscientious soul why she should be nailed to this particular cross. Each year winter was barely out before members of the family could correctly attribute to her furrowed brow the passage of such an unspoken thought as 'I wonder if I could ask Mrs Deven to take on the cake stall this year,' or 'Who will run the coconut shy now that old Vance has had his leg off?' The second reason was simply one of tradition. Since time immemorial (though actually only since about 1880) there had always been a fête at Rawle even in the war years and therefore there should always be one. Not to hold one would be equivalent to cancelling Ascot or the Boat Race. Such things marked the passing of the seasons, held together the social fabric and provided fixed points in a shifting and modernising world. They should therefore by no means be abandoned.

But there was more to it than mere tradition. There was something special about the Rawle fête that distinguished it from the common run of such events. It possessed the conventional features such as tombolas and raffles, guess the weight of the pig, throw a quoit round a peg in the grass, catapult a balloon with marbles and so on. And there was a redoubtable tea-tent. But the pièce de résistance was the quarry slide.

At some point there had been acquired from somewhere a large quantity of good wooden flooring. This came not in the form of single boards but sizeable whole sections six foot or more square, the individual boards being clamped together by means of battens underneath. Perhaps it was the floor of a ballroom of a mansion condemned to demolition, nobody quite knew, not that it mattered for it was now 'the slide'. Throughout the rest of the year it occupied an entire loose box in the stable yard which could otherwise have been put to a more regular and immediate use but such was its status in this important annual event no one begrudged it the grandeur of its quarters, as if it were a prize pig. People came to the fête from miles around entirely on the strength of this entertaining feature and it generated by direct and indirect income more than all the other entertainments put together (if you excluded the teas). Someone had suggested having the slide in permanent operation as part of the Rawle attraction but this was frowned on. 'Rawle isn't to be turned into a fairground,' was the prevailing view.

Its annual transporting, its installation, operation and subsequent dismantling were in the hands of Milton, the woodman, and his assistant Mike Osney and their team of helpers, membership of which was honourable. On account of the slide the fête took place not on the lawn in front of the house as it might otherwise have done but on a pleasant piece of green sward the other side of the lake a little short of Hangar Wood, for it was just inside the wood that there was to be found the quarry essential to the functioning of the slide. Left to itself this quarry, the stone from which had built the house it was said, would have become overgrown with brambles and elder, overshadowed by the fir trees that flourished in the sandy soil, but the designers and layers of the slide had created a track for it down the old quarry's steeply and unevenly sloping bank, as a skiing piste is sliced out of an alpine forest though not of course of such extent.

The quarry being of sandstone there was from year to year some shift and erosion to be negotiated by the pioneers, stretches of the track in need of shoring up with logs or the ground levelled. Sometimes timber piles had to be driven into the ground and even ropes, slung over substantial fir branches and secured with pegs, had to be brought into play. All this care and expertise and trouble was in the cause of safety and a smooth ride. A certain unneveness as the riders, clutching the canvas handles at the leading edge of their mats, passed over a joint between sections was acceptable in imparting an additional frisson to the experience – no more than the light click of a train's wheels passing from one piece of track to the next (ker-klunk, ker-klunk) regular and reassuring, but no more than that. A jolt, however, that might unnerve the riders was to be avoided, much more so a bump that could unseat and spill them in spite of the containing rims at the track's edge. Considerable speeds were attained and injuries had been sustained in the past though none serious enough to call the whole operation into question given how much fun and excitement it afforded regardless of the money it raised.

On the day of the fête Johnny was on duty at the bookstall as befitted his literary leanings. There was not much business and his mind went back to the morning.

It was a fine one and Fi and he found themselves breakfasting together early. Then they agreed to go for a walk before committing the rest of the day to the fête. The dogs were already out with someone so they were on their own. The day was lovely enough for them not to need to be doing any more than just enjoying it – no destination or purpose was required. At first anyway. They went down by the church (in aid of which the fête was being held) then across the lake stream and out of the park into the fields where brown cattle regarded them speculatively. The further they walked the more oppressive the situation became to Johnny. It seemed daft to be so alone with Fi but to be saying little – nothing of any consequence anyway. Why were they doing this? Why were they together, side by side, steering the same route without even having to discuss where they were going or what turns they should take? Was this companionship? What was the point of it? After a while neither nature nor desultory conversation seemed enough to fill the great space in which they moved.

Then something happened. In a corner shaded by a great oak some creature seemed to be moving on the ground. 'Oh, look – a fox!' Odd it wasn't running away with that I-don't-trust-you-but-you-can't-catch-me confidence of its kind. They approached. The animal seemed to be rolling like a dog intent on getting some dubious scent well smeared on to its shoulder. It would get up and then turn its shoulder down and roll again. It saw them with its upturned eye and there was fear in it. Then it became clear that it wanted to get away but couldn't.

Something was dragging it down as each time it got up.

'Oh God, it's hurt,' said Fi, 'and it's no more than a cub.'

'Is it caught in a trap?' Johnny queried.

'No, there's something wrong with it,' Fi replied.

'What do we do then?' This was Fi's domain after all, animals, particularly sick animals. 'Catch it and get it to the vet?'

'It won't let us catch it and the vet would only have one answer for it.'

'So we put it out of its misery here?'

'Yes, if we can get close enough.'

They stood a while and watched the animal as if it might resolve the situation itself either by dying without their having to do anything or perhaps recovering and running away. Either of those results, Johnny thought, would be just fine. One thing they couldn't do was walk away. The fox was now bouncing around in the grass as if periodically electrified – inert one moment then suddenly springing into the air. The two approached. It was clear that it was not going to run away, nor did it seem on the point of death.

'We'll need a stick,' said Fi.

A branch Johnny soon found under the oak was too rotten for the job but he went further afield, glancing over his shoulder hoping that Fi would call out to tell him there was no longer any need of his stick or of what he was going to have to do with it. He found something stouter and returned. The fox-cub was lying still, one brown eye fixed in their direction. Fi was looking down at it.

'Shall I…?' Johnny queried.

Fi wasn't offering to take the stick from him. This was going to have to be his job. He approached to do the deed. Where exactly should he hit it? – just 'over the head', he supposed. Better circle round a bit to get a better angle at the back of its head, that must be the place. Right. He raised the stick. Then suddenly the animal gave a great lurch and hurled itself up into the air as if in a frantic bid to escape what it knew was coming. Johnny was taken aback for a moment but the animal had only succeeded in hurling itself into a patch of low nettles where it collapsed. There it lay still. That was its last effort surely.

It could do no more. Johnny approached and swinging the stick high brought it down on the fox's head. The animal was partly concealed in the nettles and Johnny's blow was partly on target but some of the force was taken by the ground so he raised the stick again and this time clubbed it full-on. At that the animal's back legs thrashed violently, ripping at the nettles, as if desperate to speed away from the scene. But then they stilled, gently folding back and down to rest on the ground as if settling in sleep. And then it looked very dead. One more blow to be sure? Johnny wondered. No. Fi came up and looked down at the creature. Its one visible eye was closed.

'Come on,' she said.

Johnny dropped the stick where he stood as if it were bloodied daggers and they walked out of the shade back into the sun. Fi was quiet.

'Do you think it had escaped from a trap or something?' Johnny asked, needing to talk about it as they went.

'More like wounded by shot,' answered Fi. 'Or diseased. The crows'll have it now.'

Johnny felt as if he'd been part of something bad but done something good. He was confused, excited; he felt strong. Fi seemed unmoved but if anything more subdued. Was she upset? She loved animals and hated to see them suffer.

At the next stile, as Johnny stood aside to let Fi over first, she put her hand lightly on his shoulder as she stepped up. Getting over himself, Johnny paused a moment above her. She was still, beneath him, waiting, looking vaguely about her but not moving on.

How did you go about to hold hands? Well, there was no other way – you just did it. So he would do it.

He wondered, as so often, what she might be thinking. It might be that she was longing for him to take hold of her, that she was perhaps growing impatient with him for not acting. Before, he had been uncertain, wondering whether if he left it long enough the contact would somehow happen of its own accord like two great magnets drawn together by the invisible force within them. Perhaps if they touched naturally from time to time they would just find themselves getting together like climbing plants intertwining in mutual need, no deliberate taking and holding required. But that didn't happen. Perhaps, even, she might make the move. But no, she wouldn't and didn't and it wouldn't have been right if she had. It was a job for him. Not that he had any reason to think she might welcome it – no reason at all, it was not as if she had said or done anything that gave him any encouragement; he just felt somehow sure that he and she wanted one another – it wasn't a matter of reason but of inner leaning, of plain attraction. He knew now he wanted her and therefore that she wanted him. It was simple.

And now he knew it would happen, that he would make it happen. He felt very relaxed and sure. There was no hurry. Why rush spring because you're anxious for summer? 'The threshold is the place to pause.'

Johnny glanced down at the little hand, relishing the fact of his imminent possession. Then he took it with unmistakeable intent, though without look or word; the hand allowed itself to be taken, not with any gesture of surrender or answering grasp, but simply. Johnny could hardly breathe, let alone speak. He took possession of her hand, threading his fingers through hers which parted one by one, opening up to his and so they intertwined, fingers folding themselves over the backs of their hands, locked. Johnny did not turn her to face him and she did not turn to him. He did not seek to hold her or kiss her. They carried on as before but now connected, bound together. And so they swung along.

'I think it's time you had a tea break, Johnny. I'll hold the fort for you.'

It was Lady Nidd coming up to his bookstall.

'Oh, thanks. Not doing a lot of business,' said Johnny. 'Fi's busy, I expect.' He just wanted to say her name.

'Scones going like hot cakes,' said Lady Nidd, smiling. Her pre-show nerves had completely lapsed now that the fête was in full swing and obviously going well, and she went about chatting to all and sundry with aristocratic benignity.

The tea tent was army surplus, supported by as many ropes and stays, it seemed, as the Lilliputians required to tie down Gulliver. The interior was low, cavernous and stuffy and there

Fi was hard at work. 'I'm keeping my head down,' she said. 'Cousin Rupert's about!'

'I'll try and draw him off for you.'

'Thanks.'

Lord Nidd, as head of a family wider than the denizens of Rawle, operated on the principle of *famille oblige* however poor, disagreeable or sycophantic any cousin might be ; to him personality was unimportant, blood was all. Cousin Rupert, though described by Onjon as 'Nobody's favourite person but his own', had none of those particular defects but he was the sort to give the upper classes a bad name with his braying voice and air of superiority. On this occasion he was attired in cricket whites, cravat and matching blazer in colours discordant and virulent enough to curdle cream at fifty paces.

'Hullo, Rupert. Didn't know there was a cricket match on.'

'There isn't – not here anyway. Just popped over from Tabby's – old boys' match.'

'What's Tabby's?'

'Talbots, you ignoramus. Christ! I thought you were supposed to be a schoolmaster. Never heard of Talbots?'

'Course I have. Everybody's heard of Talbots.'

'I should say so – great school. So where are you teaching now then? Fi seemed a bit vague when I asked her the other day. Where is she, by the way? I haven't seen her. Hiding out as usual, I expect.'

'Oh, she's around.'

'Grown into quite a girl, wouldn't you say?'

'You asked about my teaching. Truth is at the moment –'

'You know what – you should teach at a place like Tabby's. Benders was just saying at lunch what a job it is getting halfway decent beaks nowadays. Chaps like you – public school, Oxford – tend to go off to the city and suchlike – like me.' (guffaw) 'Teaching just gets the leftovers, grammar school boys and people from provincial universities but it needs quality. Want me to see if there's anything going in your line – English, isn't it? – when I get back?'

'The headmaster's name is Benders?'

'Well, Bendinck actually. Quite human for a head man – no disappearing trick from a man like him, unlike this character at the funny little school on the Isle of Wight. I expect you read about it.'

'Yes, I –'

'Probably up to no good. Usually is. Fiddling the books or fiddling the boys. Still the police'll get it out of him, I expect.'

'If they get him, that is,' said Johnny, ashamed (like Peter) at his disloyalty.

'What do you mean "get him"? They've got him.'

'What!'

'Yes. In the paper today.'

'I haven't seen the –'

'In Singapore, apparently. No full story yet, of course, but looks like he stowed away or bribed his way on to a ship at Southampton bound for New Zealand. Some one turned him over when they docked. He'll be back in England soon. "The Runaway Headmaster" – the press must be thrilled to get some life back into this one. They love stories to do with public schools – if you can call his odd little establishment a public school, not that it's still in business of course, few schools could survive a scandal like that, even without the gory details of why the man hopped it in the first place. Anyway, as I was saying, I'll put in a word for you with Benders if you like.'

Johnny was slow to answer. 'I don't suppose that at this stage of the year he'd have any vacancy; he'll be all set up for September.'

'You never know, he might have something going, no harm in asking, I say. Want me to mention it?'

'Well –' (Come on idiot, how choosy can you afford to be?) 'thanks, that would be –'

'No trouble. Catch up with you later.'

Cousin Rupert departed, licking cream from his fat fingers.

Talbot College? thought Johnny. Cousin Rupert's old school! If Cousin Rupert was a typical product of the place how could he even think about it? On the other hand, if he was a typical product of the place – well, it was time somebody did something about it! – and why not him, Johnny Clarke, who'd learnt a thing or two over the last year. Yes, this 'Tabby's' could probably do with a shot of Clouds and he would bloody well deliver it if he got the chance.

Then Fi was at his elbow.

`Come on,' she said, 'let's have a go on the slide.'

'They've found Minkie,' he told her. 'I wonder if it'll be possible to talk to him, when they bring him back to England, if that's what they're going to do.'

'Well, probably. He'll need his friends whatever happens.'

Yes, thought Johnny, we need our friends whatever happens. But how far are you prepared to go for them?

'Slide?' repeated Fi, this time looking up into his face.

Johnny had already contemplated this possibility and decided against it, taking refuge behind his bookstall. If he was a conscientious helper, he reasoned to himself, he couldn't be expected to dash about with a handful of sixpences tasting all the fun of the fair. Leave that to the customers – he had a duty. On setting up the day before Johnny had seen something of what was in store and it had not attracted him; the team at work on the slide might as well have been setting up a scaffold. Then he had actually at the start of the proceedings spent a minute or two standing at the bottom of it watching the first intrepid 'tobogganists' arriving at its level termination, tumbling over the expanse of cushioned matting laid out to take their fall, as it were on the other side of the high jump. The thrill in their eyes! But Johnny had also been up at the top and looked down the slide and that was quite another matter – in fact in his opinion bloody terrifying. But he had descended on foot, comforting himself with the thought that there would be no pressure on him to take that dreadful dive. He was an adult permitted to make his own choices. He had no head for heights, anyway, he told himself. It wasn't a matter of 'scaredy, scaredy', it was a condition, like hay fever, you couldn't be expected…

'Come on!' She took his hand. He had no choice.

'Oh, OK!'

Toiling up the sandy slope through the trees Johnny's heart was a mixture of dread and excitement. He truly feared heights: ladders, high windows, cliff-tops, bridges – anywhere that a false step or an uncontrolled inclination could spell a headlong and fatal descent. As a boy he had been expected to climb church towers: the horrible dark closeness of the spiral staircase dimly and occasionally lit by the slit windows, each one as he ascended offering a more terrible separation from the homely ground. Then emergence into daylight on the roof was a blessed escape from that confinement but also a dreadful exposure to too much uncaring sky and the terror that his own demon could rise within him and hurl him from the heights. Now he knew before he got there the precipitous brown sweep of the slide, at the bottom the faces of the gormless onlookers, the *tricoteuses* complacently licking ice creams as luckless heads rolled at their feet. How he longed to be one of them, safe and sound, a spectator of life rather than a participant! Or were some of them envious? Were they not perhaps themselves hungry for the exhilaration of those who tumbled happily before them, faces alight with glee, with excitement and pride in fear overcome? Were they, these onlookers, for all their smug safety, ashamed of their own timidity, living in the pusillanimous comfort of the grandstand, never in the pavilion padded up for action on the square, never scoring, safe from the spectacle of a fast bowler bearing down upon them and safe from the ignominy of a duck but their ears never blessed by the sound of applause ? The missers-out.

What a huge temptation it had been to say No to Fi, to retreat behind his bookstall, making a useful contribution to the fundraising that was after all the principal purpose of the day – but never having a go on the main thing, the slide, the principal attraction. Now Fi had asked him and he had not said No and she led on.

The queue at the top was mercilessly short and their turn soon came. Yes, they were a double – large mat, please. Frisky coconut matting to sit on. Canvas handles on the leading edge for front man to hold up and cling on to. The officials so calm, so matter-of-fact: 'You on properly? OK, feet in a bit.' Perhaps you got used to being an executioner, it's a routine life like any other. Now who would go at the front – him or her? Courtesy and male pride propelled Johnny forward, terror dragged him back. 'I'll go at the front,' said Fi, doing so. Thank God. 'Hold on.' What to? There was only her to hold on to. 'Put your arms round me'. Her bottom was tucked in between his legs, his chest against her back, his face in her hair, his arms round her waist. 'Ready?' No, no!

They were off. Hard hands gave them a shove-start and the treacherous mat whistled over the shiny boards, now and again nudging the containing rim, Fi pulling on the straps as on the reins of a horse with the bit between its teeth, her hair lashing in his half-closed eyes. Was there no limit to speed? Did not physics declare that given substantial friction and not too steep an angle of descent the momentum would be restrained? But no such law was applying now as their pace picked up, as the pitch suddenly steepened and they swooshed round the cambered curve to enter the last ghastly straight. But it was the last. The end was in sight. It was rushing at them certainly as if the ride were determined to do for them before it had fully run its allotted course. But there below was the little group of pitiful onlookers, standing well back from the spread of cushioned mats that awaited the brave, the achievers, the ones whose faces glowed with excitement and whose hearts swelled with triumph. He and she were as good as there. Then suddenly from the group of spectators a small child detached itself and set off across the crash mats to someone on the other side. They were headed straight for it. With a fierce last-second jerk Fi yanked on the right handle of the mat and they spun off sideways, missing the toddler by inches, the two of them spilling helplessly off their sleigh and coming to rest in a jumbled heap, half-on, half-off the cushioning. One moment, as it seemed to Johnny, they were careering down the slide and the next he was prostrate on the ground, his arms still clasped if anything more tightly round the waist of his partner. Her hands clasped his hands. He was experiencing now two exquisite and contrasting sensations, one of pain and one of pleasure. His right knee, as he made gently to move it, shot red-hot arrows up through his body, but his left cheek was at rest on Fi's.

'You all right?' he felt her mouth say beside his.

'No. Yes. You?'

She moved her cheek gently beneath his.

'Oh yes, yes.'

'I love you,' he said.

'Good.'

'Do you love me?'

'I do. I do.'

'Oh, good. Ouch!'

The next morning he was sitting on the terrace in the sun, immobilised; his knee was nowhere ready to forgive him for the accident. Fi, who had supported him around the place since had deposited him there, and gone off to do things with animals. 'I can't carry you all the time,' she'd said. To save him going upstairs they made up a bed for him on the library sofa and there he slept. Fi had leaned over him to kiss him goodnight. This had taken quite a long time.

'I told you she fancied you,' said Onjon.

'When did you tell me?'

'Years ago.'

'Oh. Will she forgive me for taking so long over it?'

'She'll forgive you anything.'

'I hope so. I might need it.'

Shout from the house: 'Johnny, a call for you. It's Cousin Rupert.'

'Oh God!'

'Shall I take it?' offered Onjon. He did and returning said, 'Seems Talbot College are in urgent need of an English master. You should ring the head on Monday if you're interested.'

So it was that Johnny found himself talking to a spaniel about his ideas on education.

And so it was too that one cold January day the following year Frith was called upon to don his white gloves and be master of ceremonies at the wedding.

'Pray silence,' he boomed, 'for the father of the bride, Lord Nidd'.

'My Lords, Ladies and Gentlemen – and I am pleased and proud to include among such lords temporal as your humble servant before you a peer of greater distinction, being no less than a lord spiritual though as yet denied a seat in the House that he would undoubtedly fill with greater distinction than the rows of hereditary nincompoops like myself. I refer of course to the father of the groom, the Right Reverend Matthew Clarke who as you have just witnessed has solemnised this matrimony.' (Widespread murmurs of appreciation. Johnny's father beams above his purple, one hand on his pectoral cross, the other clasping a champagne glass, charged for the coming toast.) 'A warm welcome to him and of course his wife Phoebe – why she isn't a 'lady' to his 'lord' I'm not clear but that's the C. of E. for you, or the College of Heralds or whoever it is that decides these vital matters. In welcoming your son – another John to add to this family of Johns – I welcome you.' (More warm murmurs.)

'Many of you know how close Johnny has been to Rawle since he and our own Onjon met at Oxford. He has been a good friend to us all and nothing gives me greater pleasure than to hand over to his loving care my younger daughter, Fiona. It so happens I once facetiously offered him her hand in marriage but he had other things on his mind at the time and other adventures to attend to before coming round to this highly sensible course of action. He is a sound lad and does the right thing in the end.' (Laughter.) 'So it was a fine and ironic moment when last summer he came to me asking for my daughter's hand in marriage. Now the easy answer was, ' Why of course, dear boy, if she'll have you,' but you know we fathers don't get opportunities like this every day so I played along a bit with, 'And how do you propose to keep my daughter in the style to which she has been accustomed?', to which the reply was, 'I don't. I can't.' 'Indeed!' says I – mock-serious, you understand – 'have you got gainful employment?' 'Possibly,' he replies. Fortunately that 'possibly' soon turned into a 'certainly'.' (Single loud cheer from Cousin Rupert.) 'To talk of the groom is, however, the pleasure and the duty of the best man so, Onjon, we look to you for some tales out of school about our new son-in-law. We trust that they will be indiscreet and humorously discreditable. We trust – indeed request – that they not be disgraceful.' (Laughter.)

And now my daughter. (Johnny sotto voce to his bride, 'He sounds like King Lear!') Well, for a start ain't she just beautiful!' (Cries of 'Absolutely', 'Hear, hear,' 'Scrubbed up nicely', 'Good old Fi' et al.) 'Here at Rawle we're more accustomed to seeing her in jumper and jeans and her mother says that the last time this vision before you was seen in a dress was at her confirmation some seven or eight years ago.' (Laughter.) 'Be that as it may, when she came downstairs this morning I thought, Now who's this interloping glamour girl sweeping down the staircase? Is this some sort of double wedding and why haven't I been told? I swear the dogs didn't recognise her. Well, of course that was only a momentary delusion. No amount of make-up and coiffeuring, not to mention white tulle and the family diamonds (what's left of 'em) can disguise the identity of my beloved girl who – I have to add – looks so much like her own mother on her wedding day, I felt quite dizzy.' (Cheers and laughter.)

'Now I mentioned that I had once facetiously offered my daughter in marriage. As if Fi would allow herself to be offered to anyone! No, our Fi is above all a woman of her own mind. When it was time for her to follow in her sister's footsteps to Benenden did she want to go? No. Could she be persuaded?' (Cheerful cries of 'No!') 'Could she be cajoled, coerced or even bribed to go?' ('No' yet louder) 'No indeed – she was to stay at Rawle. Rawle was home and at Rawle she would remain and so she has. No boarding school for her, no university, none of this wandering around the world that seems to be the fashion amongst the young nowadays. But sticking here is not stick-in-the-mud for Fi – it's not retreating from the world, it's taking *on* the world. All you here, our family, our friends, our neighbours know what terrific work she and her brother have done to pull the old place round, to make it work as a business, to be productive and a good employer – in short an ornament to the county and an example to the country of what can be achieved by those of us lucky enough to own a decent patch of old England. I well remember that summer's evening at dinner – ooh, little more than three years ago – that my son and younger daughter first put to Lady Nidd and me their crackpot ideas about dredging lakes and letting the shooting and converting haylofts and I don't know what-all. While Onjon was putting the arguments so cogently Fi just sat there barely saying a word but chewing away at her napkin! And naturally I'm up on my high horse about all this, the son-and-heir – all of twenty years old, mark you – presuming to tell his revered father how to run the place, but I was listening to his argument and inside I was thinking, The boy's on to something here. But I was also looking at my daughter, her young jaws working away at that napkin and I thought, If there's that much conviction, that much determination behind this it's got be a runner with a damned good chance of getting its head out in front. And so it has proved. Bless you, my girl.' (Lord Nidd turns to his daughter, paternal sentiment clouding his vision.)

'Now that's all very well' (speaker recovering himself) 'but in case you hadn't noticed, my darling girl – yes, I'm talking to you, leave that young man alone a minute, you've got him for life so there'll be plenty of other opportunities to attend to him – you are now married and will no doubt wish to follow the declaration of your second namesake, Ruth, that "whither thou goest I shall go" – the "thou" in this case being your husband, of course. And it is said that "for this cause shall a man leave his father and mother and shall be joined unto his wife; and they two shall be one flesh." Now I take that to mean t'other way round as well – correct me if I'm wrong, Bishop – and therefore that the woman shall likewise leave father and mother and cleave to her man. So, girl, you're hitched up to his star from now on and it's off to married quarters at Talbot College with you!

Not that that's so terrible, of course, the aforesaid establishment being barely twenty minutes away so I dare say we'll be seeing a lot of you even perhaps in term time if your lord and master permits it, and of course in the absurdly long holidays that schoolmasters get, when you will be making yourselves snug on the top floor of this house or somewhere – until such time, that is, that family developments call for more expansive quarters.' (Bride hides blushing face; rude cheers from younger male guests.) 'Till then, my darling girl, be you a good wife to your good man. My Lords, Ladies and Gentlemen, I give you this toast' – (Frith, a champagne bottle in white-gloved hand scans crowd for any empty glasses) – '"The bride!" '

'The bride!'

8

TALBOT COLLEGE 4

The Flat

Morrison's
Talbot College
Berks

Jan 22nd

Dear Mum and Dad,

It's good you were able to see this place so you don't need me to describe it to you, though things are somewhat different of course during term when the boys are around, as Fi has discovered a little to her dismay, though she is good about it. When I say it would have been nicer not to be right above a dormitory she replies that it's better than being right below one! Considering a dormitory is a place for sleeping you'd be surprised how much noise comes out of it – sometimes you'd think they were playing rugby in there which come to think of it they possibly are – and I suppose it's only to be expected that if you put sixty boys in one room it's bound to be noisy from time to time.

What is great, though, is having this little place to ourselves. Boys do sometimes come to the door but that's the limit and we love having our privacy, surrounded with all our wonderful wedding presents. Fi says it's like living in a department of Peter Jones! Boarding school being what it is, I am working all the hours God gave – and quite a few he didn't! On my duty night, for example, admittedly only one night a week, I'm on the go till gone eleven by which time Fi has called it a day and gone to bed so there are the odd days when we hardly see each other at all, though as I remind her it beats commuting.

It's not an ideal life for Fi, of course, because until now her whole life was Rawle and now here she has no role as well as being separated from her beloved home. Well, we've got round that problem by her going over there from time to time and occasionally staying overnight when there's some pressure on there or the weather's foul for driving in the dark only to find I'm not in the flat anyway because it's Politics Society night and she might as well have stayed over. Rawle is and always will be immensely important to her and I'm not going to stand in the way of that. It's important to me too and we both hope that before long we may get a little bit of the place to call our own. It's too early to say what or where that might be but we have our eye on somewhere. During term of course I can't get over at all, either day or night, but in the holidays it will be our real home and we're hugely looking forward to that.

I know I have thanked you both for your love and kindness and generosity over the wedding but I don't know that I have thanked you for your love and kindness and generosity over the years, throughout my life, in fact. Of course I've taken it for granted, as I suppose children naturally do, that their parents will provide for them and perhaps more importantly always be on their side and wanting the best for them. You certainly have for me and I am so grateful.

Gratitude is something I feel so fully at the moment as you may well imagine. I still feel in a bit of a daze about being married and about Fi loving me and me loving her. It has come like a wonderful bolt from the blue, like digging away in the vegetable plot and suddenly turning up a golden crown! It seems extraordinary that having known her for years it is only now that I have <u>seen</u> her. How could I have not noticed her? How could I not have recognised the feeling I had for her underneath that it took just a slight accident or the right moment to bring out before my eyes? Yes, 'the scales fell from his eyes'! it was like a sudden conversion, a vision, that supersedes everything else, sweeps it aside in a glorious wave. I could look at her all day and when she's not at home I feel I can tell just as soon as I walk in the door, there is a kind of emptiness or chill there. But then I know she will be coming back and my heart warms again and I purr quietly to myself like a cat!

Well, enough for now – must rush – I don't think all my letters will be as emotional as this one but as you can tell I am very happy and feel very lucky. And I owe you so much. In haste.

Your loving son, Johnny.

The new assistant English master at Talbot College grabbed his new gown, slung it over the shoulder of his new sports jacket and joined the throng in the cloisters headed for chapel. The bell was ringing.

THE END

The first book in
THE SONS OF THE MORNING
sequence is
A STORM OF CHERRIES

In this story, Johnny Clarke rises to the challenges of being Head Boy at his prep school, The Dell. With a demanding headmaster, a strong rival, a strange boy and an assistant master who does what he shouldn't, his job is not an easy one; but, inspired by the beautiful new matron, he sees it through to a triumphant conclusion, though the fate of the school and of its headmaster is not so rosy.

Popular Praise for

A STORM OF CHERRIES

'… everything is as I remember it. You negotiate between the ironic and affectionate with considerable skill, and … what really impresses me is the way in which you manage to recreate the child's eye view … I'm much looking forward to the further adventures of Johnny Clarke.' *John Mole*

'It all brings back my preparatory school days. Happy as they were, all the masters are living in your book.' *Peter Gormley*

'Very easy reading and compulsive to the end … you were describing exactly my prep school and most of my experiences.'
Jack Thomas

'Incredibly well-observed stuff: I loved it. I am very much looking forward to the rest of the series.' *Nicholas Patterson*

'It is a fine piece of work: funny, deft, sad and spot-on true … you have caught brilliantly the world of prep schools as they were.'
Quentin Letts

'I was captivated by the story and the reminiscences it produced.'
Matthew Forster

The second book in
THE SONS OF THE MORNING
sequence is
DANCING DAYS

It is 1960 and the Headmaster declares that Worthington College is to admit girls into the Sixth Form. An outrage or an opportunity? Johnny Clarke and his friends in the Lower Sixth are not sure, particularly in view of the unpopular master put in charge of the development. But when Johnny falls in love at the school dance his mind is all on his beloved – until there emerges from one man's cupboard a skeleton that threatens the young lovers' happiness.

Popular Praise for

DANCING DAYS

' 'Dancing Days' brilliantly captures the innocence and sophistication that is the essence of privileged youth.'
TIM RICE, lyricist

'... several friends at school – agree that it is a fascinating insight into a life that is both so fundamentally different and yet so very similar to the ones we lead at boarding school today.'
THOMAS CLAYTON, Wykehamist

'A beautifully told tale ...'
PETER ATTENBOROUGH, formerly headmaster Charterhouse School.

'I found it wonderfully readable and hilariously perceptive.'
ADAM TYLER, former pupil at the Royal Grammar School, Guildford.

'You bring to life the nearly claustrophobic atmosphere of the public school community as it was but the characters are timeless and the story compulsive.'
RICHARD FIELD, formerly housemaster, Shrewsbury School.

'...You do have a wonderful insight into the minds of the young ...'
IAN BEER, formerly Headmaster Lancing College and Harrow School

The third book in
THE SONS OF THE MORNING
sequence is
THE LAST ENCHANTMENTS

The stirring events of 1962-3 – the Cuban missile crisis, the long hard winter, the Profumo scandal and the dramatic rise of the Beatles – culminating in the assassination of President Kennedy provide the background to The Last Enchantments. Britain is wriggling out of its post-war chrysalis but at the same time the heritage of old England must be fought for – and saved ...

Popular Praise for

THE LAST ENCHANTMENTS

'An entertaining blend of fact and fiction about university life places Simon Watson's *The Last Enchantments* in the fine tradition of the Oxford novel.'
Dr Michael Vaughan-Lee, Professor of Mathematics, Oxford University

'It has everything – women, politics, sport, faith ... for me it's way the best of the trilogy.'
The Rev Canon Julian Reindorp, Vicar of Richmond, Surrey

' You write with enviable fluency, clarity and humour.'
Quentin Letts, journalist

' ... pinpoint accuracy in evoking the world-within-world of Oxford in the early sixties ... I like your unashamed romanticism.'
John Rayner, formerly Head of English, Gresham's School, Holt.

'It really does capture the 'Oxbridge' of the sixties.'
Brigadier R.C. Wolverson

'...The third highly exciting, evocative and satisfying read ...'
Steve Benson, formerly Headmaster Bishops Stortford College, Herts.

The fourth book in
THE SONS OF THE MORNING
sequence is
A TOUCH OF THE SUN

A year in India is a ride on a tiger for Johnny Clarke. Fresh from Oxford and grappling with the challenges of teaching in an alien land, he finds himself perilously caught up in military and political events, in espionage and warfare. How can he motivate his reluctant students? Can he save his hot-headed star pupil from self-destruction? And how is he to cope with his passion for a married woman?

Popular Praise for

A TOUCH OF THE SUN

'Johnny's adventures ring true...One finds oneself turning the pages of one's own life – how it might have been as much as how it was.' *(John Mole)*

'India comes across with all its contrasts, all its layers and levels of human experience.' *(Richard Poulton)*

'*A Touch of the Sun* is more than just a good read. It is also troublingly, unnervingly true.' *(Quentin Letts)*

'What I enjoyed most was the love story which I thought was delicately done.' *(John Dancy)*

'Simon Watson has a sharp eye for the local detail of Northern India. He creates lively characters and puts them in a remarkable variety of scenes. For a well-told, well-paced and often very amusing read, this novel comes highly recommended.'
(Catherine Moorehead)